NOV 02 2018

A NOVEL BASED ON THE LIFE OF

HENRY MANCINI

GRACE NOTES

Stacia Raymond

WILLARD LIBRARY, BATTLE CREEK, MI

Grace Notes is a work of fiction. Some incidents, dialogue, and characters are products of the author's imagination and are not to be construed as real. Where real-life historical figures appear, the situations, incidents, and dialogue concerning those persons are based on or inspired by actual events. In all other respects, any resemblance to actual persons, living or dead, events, or locales is entirely coincidental.

Barbera Foundation, Inc.
P.O. Box 1019
Temple City, CA 91780

Copyright © 2018 Barbera Foundation, Inc.
Cover photo: Pictorial Press Ltd / Alamy Stock Photo
Cover design: Suzanne Turpin

More information at www.mentorisproject.org

ISBN: 978-1-947431-14-0

Library of Congress Control Number: 2018949596

All rights reserved, which includes the right to reproduce this book or portions thereof in any form whatsoever except as provided by the U.S. Copyright Law. For information address Barbera Foundation, Inc.

All net proceeds from the sale of this book will be donated to Barbera Foundation, Inc. whose mission is to support educational initiatives that foster an appreciation of history and culture to encourage and inspire young people to create a stronger future.

The Mentoris Project is a series of novels and biographies about the lives of great Italians and Italian-Americans: men and women who have changed history through their contributions as scientists, inventors, explorers, thinkers, and creators. The Barbera Foundation sponsors this series in the hope that, like a mentor, each book will inspire the reader to discover how she or he can make a positive contribution to society.

Contents

Foreword

First and foremost, Mentor was a person. We tend to think of the word *mentor* as a noun (a mentor) or a verb (to mentor), but there is a very human dimension embedded in the term. Mentor appears in Homer's *Odyssey* as the old friend entrusted to care for Odysseus's household and his son Telemachus during the Trojan War. When years pass and Telemachus sets out to search for his missing father, the goddess Athena assumes the form of Mentor to accompany him. The human being welcomes a human form for counsel. From its very origins, becoming a mentor is a transcendent act; it carries with it something of the holy.

The Barbera Foundation's Mentoris Project sets out on an Athena-like mission: We hope the books that form this series will be an inspiration to all those who are seekers, to those of the twenty-first century who are on their own odysseys, trying to find enduring principles that will guide them to a spiritual home. The stories that comprise the series are all deeply human. These books dramatize the lives of great Italians and Italian-Americans whose stories bridge the ancient and the modern, taking many forms, just as Athena did, but always holding up a light for those living today.

Whether in novel form or traditional biography, these

books plumb the individual characters of our heroes' journeys. The power of storytelling has always been to envelop the reader in a vivid and continuous dream, and to forge a link with the subject. Our goal is for that link to guide the reader home with a new inspiration.

What is a mentor? A guide, a moral compass, an inspiration. A friend who points you toward true north. We hope that the Mentoris Project will become that friend, and it will help us all transcend our daily lives with something that can only be called holy.

—Robert J. Barbera, President, Barbera Foundation
—Ken LaZebnik, Editor, The Mentoris Project

Prologue

On a trip to Pennsylvania in 1988 to conduct the Pittsburgh Symphony Orchestra, Henry Mancini felt an unmistakable tug luring him back to West Aliquippa, the town where he'd grown up. It had been decades since Henry had been back to see what had become of the place where his life and musical journey began. The musician friends traveling with him from Los Angeles were happy to accompany their beloved bandleader on the impromptu roots trip.

Henry shared some of his personal history with his companions on the drive. He told them how West Aliquippa was once a thriving steel town where the Jones and Laughlin Steel Company employed the majority of the town's residents, including his father. It was not unlike other Rust Belt towns of that era, filled with hard-working immigrant families. As they pulled into what was left of the town, it was clear that Henry had not prepared himself for the level of economic devastation that had befallen West Aliquippa, which seemed to have been reduced to dust and broken glass. There were no people on the street—just a feral cat that darted out in front of their car.

They drove around until Henry was able to trace his steps back to Beaver Avenue, which took longer than it should have because things were not all where they used to be. As they turned a corner, he felt a bit disoriented as he searched for numbers on the houses. Then he finally found it: 401, his childhood home. It was here that he lived with his parents, Quinto and Anna, who had immigrated to America from Italy. The car came to a stop and Henry got out slowly, cautiously approaching the modest clapboard structure that once held all his dreams. He never would have expected this experience to affect him so deeply. As he slowly sat on the front steps, memories came back to him in a flood, like the one that nearly wiped out the entire town when he was a boy. He remembered sitting on this same front step watching houses wash downriver, animals clinging to the roofs for dear life. He hadn't thought about that in a long time.

After a few moments, they returned to the car and drove further into town. Henry wanted to see if Aliquippa High School was still standing, although he was doubtful the town had enough people left to sustain it. But as the car pulled up to the school, Henry was encouraged to see signs of life. Flanked by his fellow musicians, he entered through the front doors and found his way to the music room, where his eyes were drawn to a little spinet piano—a smaller and much less expensive model than a regular piano. It was the very same one he used to play all those years ago when he was a student there. He placed his fingers on the keys and closed his eyes, remembering everything . . .

Chapter One

SONS OF ITALY

Italian family life is one rich in tradition and flush with culture. The Mancini family was no different in this respect. Enrico Nicola Mancini, or "Henry" as he was called, was born to immigrant parents willing to make every sacrifice necessary to ensure a better life for their child. Despite their desire for a large family, Quinto and Anna Mancini only ever had one child. Henry was born on April 16, 1924, and was named after Quinto's brother who died in Yugoslavia in World War I. Anna suffered several miscarriages before Henry and doctors advised her not to have any more children. This came as a blow to the couple, but it also meant that every bit of their energy and attention could be poured into their beloved son. Perhaps being an only child named after an uncle who perished at a young age put a great deal of pressure on Henry to accomplish extraordinary things. And he did.

Forte piano is a musical term used to denote a mode of playing that is strong yet gentle. This may be the best way to think about Henry's father, Quinto, who was infused with a boundless love of music but was simultaneously a man of steel in two ways: a steel worker by trade, and a stoic old-world Italian who rarely showed much outward expression of love for his wife or son. He was the ultimate study in contradictions as a piccolo flute–playing steel worker.

Quinto and Anna emigrated from Abruzzo, Italy, on the coast of the magnificent Adriatic Sea. Quinto had been somewhat hardened by life by an uncle who cheated Quinto's father out of his inheritance and forced Quinto and his siblings off their father's land. A professional musician for a time, Quinto was determined to prevent his son from following his same life in the steel mills, where he found work in the new world. His dream was for Henry to go to college and earn a degree; Quinto was instrumental in this effort as Henry's first music teacher. After he'd taught his son as much as he could, Quinto sought the best instruction for him. Even at the depths of the Depression, the steel mills of West Aliquippa never stopped, and Quinto and Anna were able to scrape together the money needed to ensure their son would have the best opportunities they could possibly provide, even if that meant going without elsewhere in their lives. One winter, Anna went without an adequate overcoat so that there would be enough money for Henry's lessons.

Quinto was a strict father. As Henry's music teacher, he could be highly critical of his young son at times. When Henry was eight years old, Quinto contracted a terrible case of the mumps, which is often excruciatingly painful for an adult. One day during his illness, Quinto was stuck indoors with Henry and sent him to the closet to get two cases down from the upper shelf. Henry dragged a chair across the floor, climbed on top of it, and pulled the cases down.

"What's in here, Papa? BB guns? Butterfly nets? A telescope?"

Henry's father looked at him sternly. "We're going to put all of your excess energy to good use, boy. Handle those carefully! Put them on the table. Over here."

Henry did as he was told. Then he placed his hands on the locks and popped the first case open. Inside was a shiny flute in three separate pieces.

"That one is too big for you yet. Open the other one."

Henry popped the locks on the second case and found a similar instrument. It was about half the size of the flute.

"Are we going to play music, Papa?"

"It will take many hours of practice before you will be able to play."

This did not seem to discourage young Henry.

"Is this a child's flute?"

"It is a flautino, but most would call it a piccolo. That is not entirely correct, though, because a piccolo just means the smallest and most high-pitched of a family of instruments. So, you have your violin piccolo, piccolo clarinet, and timpani piccolo. But we are getting ahead of ourselves . . ."

Henry's first lesson began in earnest with one command from his father: "*Blow.*"

Henry blew. He blew. And he blew. But no sound came out. He continued blowing until he felt light-headed, but *still* no sound came out. Quinto was soon exhausted and fell asleep without any noise to keep him awake. Henry just kept on blowing.

It took many more lessons for Henry to develop the embouchure, or correct position of the mouth—to make any sound come out of the flautino. He learned that even this could be a misleading name because some composers used it to refer to a small recorder, making it difficult to determine for sure what they actually intended just by looking at the written music. After learning to finally coax sound out of his instrument, Henry was a fast learner and played plenty of notes, including lots of wrong ones. Whenever this happened, Quinto would reach inside their birdhouse for its wooden perch and whack Henry's fingers with it.

At school, Henry's best friend, Jack, noticed Henry's red knuckles.

"Hey, Henry," he whispered, trying not to draw the teacher's attention. "What happened to your hands?"

Henry looked down, then back at Jack. "Bar fight."

Jack could hardly stifle a laugh as the teacher looked up from her desk. This was one of many chuckles the two boys would share. Henry was always making Jack laugh with his extra-dry sense of humor. Class let out and, once they were in the hallway, Jack asked about the red knuckles again, hoping to get a straight answer this time.

"So, are you gonna tell me what really happened?"

Henry shrugged. "My father whacks my knuckles every time I play a wrong note."

"Jeez, I bet you don't make the same mistake twice!"

"I try not to."

"But you're getting so good on that little flute. Maybe I should get my father to whack my fingers when I practice trumpet."

"Give a try. But just remember, it's the patented Mancini method."

"Got it."

They laughed again heartily, running outside into the bright sunshine.

Once Henry had become a competent piccolo player, his father broke the news to him that the two of them were going to join the local Sons of Italy band.

"But I don't want to play in front of people," Henry protested.

"Nonsense," his father replied.

The Sons of Italy band played all the local graduations, parades, and games, so there was always a big audience.

"I really don't."

"You would rather waste your God-given talent?"

Henry's mother, Anna, understood that Henry could be very shy at times. "Must you be so hard on him, my dear?" she said to Quinto.

Henry turned to his mother with pleading eyes. "Why must I play in front of others, Mother?"

"When the Sons of Italy band plays on holy days, my son, it is for the glory of God. Sure, the strongest men in the town carry the saint's statue through the streets in parade, but it is the Sons of Italy band who lead the way."

"Can Jack do it too? He's getting pretty good on the trumpet. He even asked his father to whack his fingers like you do to me when he plays a wrong note."

"Is he Italian?" Quinto asked.

"No, he's Irish."

"Tell him to start a Sons of Ireland band."

Against Henry's protesting, he and his father joined the Sons of Italy band, which practiced at the Sons of Italy Hall. At first, it was just as bad as Henry expected. There he got his weekly ration of Puccini, Rossini, and Verdi. They met every Sunday at eleven a.m. after mass to rehearse. At events, Henry disliked performing in front of people even more than he thought he would, though he really didn't know why. One rare Saturday on which the band did not have an engagement, Quinto decided to take Henry to a movie theater in Pittsburgh. Henry had seen many of the silent films of Buster Keaton, Charlie Chaplin, and Laurel and Hardy, but this would be his first talkie.

They walked up to the box office, where his father paid for their tickets. As they entered the theater, Henry's eyes grew wide. He ran his hands over the plush red-velvet seats, following behind his father. Once they sat down, he felt his chin tip toward the ceiling as he marveled at all that glittered above him in vibrant colors and gold leaf. Chandeliers sparkled like objects dropped straight from heaven. Henry had never been surrounded by so much opulence and knew he was in for something special.

Just as soon as the house lights dimmed and the curtain went up, Henry heard the opening notes of a spectacular fanfare. On the screen, three knights on horseback came into view, flickering in black and white. The film title read:

The Crusades
Produced and Directed by Cecil B. DeMille

Henry thought that sounded like quite a grand name. A few seconds later, the words *Music by Rudolph Kopp* came across the screen and Henry later made sure he remembered that. The film's music was so magnificent and affective that Henry felt transported directly into the story. He was thunderstruck. The music filled up his entire being to the point that he could feel his insides vibrate. As an angry mob cheered onscreen, a group of men used ropes to pull a large cross off the top of a building and the crowd erupted when it was smashed to pieces. Henry yanked on his father's coat without taking his eyes off the screen for a second. He whispered into his father's ear, "How do they fit the whole orchestra behind the screen, Father?"

Quinto shot Henry a look in the dark and, in a dialect spoken in his native Abruzzi, answered him. "You misunderstand, *cafone*," he told Henry, using an Italian word for a rube or a dope, but Henry didn't seem to care what name he was being called. Shaking his head, Quinto tried to explain. "The orchestra is not behind the movie. It is *part* of the movie."

Henry scrunched his brow, unable to comprehend what his father was saying. He couldn't tear his eyes away from the film and wanted his father to stop talking because he just wasn't making sense. Henry decided right then and there that he wanted to write music for the movies too, even if he didn't totally understand how it was *part* of the movie.

When they returned home to West Aliquippa, Henry ran straight to Jack's house. He couldn't wait to tell him all about his marvelous experience. He breathlessly tried to explain everything he'd seen and heard.

"There were knights on horseback and the horses were draped in shiny banners. There was King Richard the Lionheart, and swords and flags and coats of arms and battles. And the *music*! You wouldn't believe it! It played almost throughout the whole movie without stopping. I thought that the orchestra was been behind the screen."

"And was it?"

"No. My father said it was *in* the movie."

"Well, if they can get talking into the movies now, maybe that's how they get the music in it too." Jack thought long and hard about this. "Oh, I know! The orchestra must play along with the actors, you know, off to the side, where the camera can't see them."

Henry began nodding his head. "Hey, why didn't I think of that?!"

The days that Henry and Jack had together to run free and play to their hearts' content were special to them because Henry was so often ill. If there were a childhood disease, it seemed that Henry was destined to catch it. One day after school when Henry was home with the chicken pox, Jack showed up at the door. Henry's mother answered.

"Hello, Jack. I'm sorry, but Henry is ill with chicken pox," she said.

"Yes, I know. My mother sent me because she wants me to catch it."

Anna Mancini was puzzled. "Some of these American customs are so strange. Very well," Anna said, ushering Jack inside.

"Besides, I have to tell Henry that I signed us both up for the school play. It's called *Babes in Toyland*. It's about these two children who run away to a magical place called Toyland and their parents have to go and search for them, but then they also get swept up in the magic of the place."

"That sounds wonderful. And that is very kind of you to sign Henry up. Maybe it will help him with his stage fright."

Jack leaned in to whisper to Mrs. Mancini, not knowing if Mr. Mancini was home from the steel mill yet. "Henry doesn't have stage fright."

"No?" Anna asked.

"He just doesn't like playing in the Sons of Italy band."

Jack smiled and strode off toward Henry's room, where he found his friend covered with red dots.

"And here I thought you might be faking," Jack told Henry. "I came to cheer you up. I volunteered us both for the school Christmas play, *Babes in Toyland*."

Henry shrugged.

"You're not mad?" Jack asked.

"Not as long as you do it too."

"I need you to keep it from getting too dull."

Quiet as Henry was, Jack always knew that Henry's silence was really just giving him time to set up his next joke. When rehearsals for the play got underway, Henry took to wearing his costume hat backwards. This got a laugh out of everyone and only encouraged Henry to continue to keep clowning. Doing *Babes in Toyland* taught Henry a very important lesson: you could goof off all you wanted in practice, but when it came time for the real performance, it was time to get serious. The night of the show, Quinto and Anna sat in the audience feeling very proud of their son.

"Perhaps he is growing out of his stage fright," Quinto whispered to Anna.

She smiled and patted him on the leg lovingly.

"His flute playing is improving greatly as well," Quinto told her. "It is possible he will surpass me soon."

Anna was surprised. She was not a musician but always thought that her husband was an impressive flautist. She would have thought it would take many years for Henry to reach his level.

"*Superare*?" She asked, using the Italian for *surpass*. "Does that mean he is better than you already?"

He gave her a stern look. He was a proud man, after all.

When Henry wasn't practicing flute or running around with Jack, he could be found at the house of a neighbor who owned a player piano. He would sit for hours, mesmerized by watching the keys move up and down on their own accord as they played

Chapter Two

MUSICAL AWAKENINGS

As if already suffering through a severe case of chicken pox weren't bad enough for young Henry, he went on to contract mumps, measles, and diphtheria. Perhaps it was these frequent illnesses that gave him more time than most kids to practice music. Even when he was too weak to play, he would listen to records on a constant loop, analyzing every note. Then the worst one of all struck when he was a young teen and he came down with rheumatic fever. Left temporarily crippled by the illness, he took to crawling on the floor. But all this time out of school and band practice didn't seem to affect his progress—he was a very fast learner, a natural leader, and was beginning to enjoy music more and more ever since he joined a larger group of peers. His flute playing soon became top notch and, in 1937, when he was only thirteen, he was named first flautist in the Pennsylvania All-State Band.

When he wasn't playing with one of his two bands, Henry was becoming fascinated with stretching his left hand to reach a ten-key span, as the legendary pianist and bandleader Count Basie was doing. Jazz had caught the ear of arrangers and given rise to the big band, which included anywhere from twelve- to twenty-four-piece ensembles. At the same time, sweeter-toned groups incorporated jazz into a more commercial style that led to the birth of swing and dance bands. As Duke Ellington described swing, "The rhythm causes a bouncy, buoyant, terpsichorean urge." This was a fancy way of saying that the music made people want to get up and dance, inspired by the muse of dancing, Terpsichore. Swing continued to evolve as big band music was becoming more frequently arranged than improvised.

Henry wanted to emulate the greats as much as humanly possible. The biggest breakthrough for swing happened when Benny Goodman, who had a legion of radio fans, purchased and began using a few dozen arrangements from Fletcher Henderson, an African-American bandleader, thereby spreading the influence of black music to a wider American public. As dance halls across the country began to fill, Goodman quickly became known as the "King of Swing," with his musical instinct and magical touch on the clarinet. Henry fell in love with this music and could not get enough—he wanted to learn everything. Luckily for Henry, he had long fingers. He spent every minute at his desk at school stretching his left thumb away from his fingers, pressing down on his desk over and over until he mastered it. Henry was incredibly inspired by the new rhythm of the double bass in the rhythm section, which produced a four-in-a-bar walking bass style instead of the two-beat stomping feel of earlier jazz. He also grew to greatly admire Goodman for pioneering musical racial integration.

These developments began to help Henry discover his

identity as a musician and as a person. Like his father, he did not suffer fools gladly. It was around this time that the school bully had started going after kids in the cafeteria at lunchtime by pounding the hands of anyone who had them on the table. Henry and Jack watched this day after day, wondering what could be done about it.

"Who does that guy think he is, running around and terrorizing everyone all lunch period long?" Henry asked Jack.

They stood with their backs against the wall thinking about it.

"Wait. I think I might have an idea," Henry said. "C'mon."

Jack followed Henry to a couple of open seats at a table. Henry was becoming lightning fast with his hands from all his piano practice. He motioned for Jack to sit down with a group of particularly vulnerable students as the bully was making his way across the room.

BAM! BAM! BAM!

The bully sailed through the room like a wrecking ball, pounding the hands of anyone who didn't see him coming.

Henry leaned over to the boy next to him and asked, "Has he been over here yet?"

The boy shook his head no.

"Perfect."

The shy boy was confused.

Henry kept a close watch on the bully from the corner of his eye, and as the tyrant moved ever closer, he stretched both arms straight up over his head to purposely draw attention to himself. Then he brought them down, casually placed both hands on top of the table, and pretended to play piano. In a bit of an exaggerated fashion, he began to whistle to himself, looking left to right, doing his best to act nonchalant. Henry could see Jack getting nervous as the bully got closer, clearly identifying Henry as his next victim.

"Henry, look out!" one of the other kids mumbled under her breath to warn him.

"Yeah, he's coming this way," said another.

As the bully came to the edge of the table and was about to pound Henry's fingers with a punishing blow, Henry yanked his hands out of the way just in time so that the bully ended up slamming his own hands *hard*. The bully howled in agony and the entire cafeteria erupted in laughter as Henry was heralded a hero.

Henry rejected any notion of himself as hero, though—not when he was just doing what he thought was right. As a rather innocent-minded young lad, his childlike presumptions about how things worked continued to unfold. Just as when he was convinced that there *had* to be an orchestra behind the movie screen at *The Crusades*, and when thought that a player piano could not be played manually, he also didn't have any reason to believe that one could buy *blank* music paper, so he'd spend hours drawing out five-line staves with a pencil and ruler. Once he had the lined paper finished, he could get to the real work, which was feverishly copying Artie Shaw arrangements from Shaw's big band recordings. Henry had become a self-described Artie Shaw nut. He became a boy obsessed with learning how the arrangements worked, to the point of getting reprimanded for working on them in school.

As a devout Catholic family, much of the Mancini's social life revolved around parish activities. One of the traditions of their church was organizing riverboat day trips. Henry had been on several of these, but when he was fourteen, he went unaccompanied by his parents for the first time. He had to wake up early to meet at St. George Byzantine, where the church bus would be waiting to transport the group to the Ohio River. They arrived at the dock and began to line up to board the vessel when Henry heard the first sounds of a band playing.

It wasn't like any live band he'd ever heard before. His keen musician ears told him that the band was only warming up, but even that made him stand at attention. Once aboard the boat, he searched the decks following the sound and found a group made up entirely of black players. As they began their first song, Henry got goose bumps. Their style was so fresh and the rhythm section so tight! It was the most electrifying music Henry had ever heard live. As the riverboat paddles began to spin, Eddie, one of Henry's friends, found him sitting as close as he could to the band.

"C'mon, we've got a game of fivestones going on the top deck," Eddie told him, using the then-common term for a game of jacks.

"I'll catch up with you in a while," Henry said.

Eddie didn't understand what he was missing. "What are you doing down here anyway?" he asked.

"Can you please stop talking? I'm trying to listen to the music."

"Suit yourself."

And that is precisely what Henry did. During the twelve-hour excursion, Henry spent at least ten hours close enough to the band to reach out and touch them. On their first break, Henry worked up the courage to talk to one of the horn players.

"Hi, my name is Henry. I, uh, just wanted to tell you how much I'm enjoying your band. I play a little myself, but *you guys*. I mean, first of all, how do you play without any sheet music?"

The horn player laughed and said, "You play through a song enough times and it just sticks, you know?"

"No. Not really. I mean, I never realized that could happen. How many times do you have to play it?" Henry asked.

"Oh, hundreds, I would guess."

"Wow."

"I'm James. What's your name, kid?"

"I'm Henry. Henry Mancini."

They shook hands.

"Nice to meet you, Henry. What do you play?"

"Flute, piccolo, and now piano too," Henry said. "I started lessons with a teacher in Pittsburgh, but it's mostly classical. And I play in the Sons of Italy band with my father. We play a lot of weddings—so, you know, polkas, Greek wedding songs, Italian folk songs. I've been teaching myself some Artie Shaw arrangements. And ragtime is my favorite, but the way you guys just lock . . . man. I didn't know music could sound so good."

"Hey, it looks like we're getting back to it here in a minute."

"Is it okay if I sit a little closer to you to hear everything? I don't want to miss a note."

"You're all right, Henry, you know that?"

They struck up the band once again and some of the players couldn't help but smile and laugh at how Henry was practically right on top of them. As the trumpet player began a solo improvisation, he looked over at young Henry, who closed his eyes, appearing as though he'd been transported to another world. At the end of each song, Henry applauded with the vigor of an entire crowd. He took pride in demonstrating for the other onlookers how to clap for solos. He'd heard this on several of the live albums he'd been studying.

When the band took another break, he went to compliment the trumpet player. James saw Henry coming with more questions.

"Hey, Jermaine. This here is Henry, a piano and flute player."

Jermaine smiled. "Is that right?"

Henry felt a little embarrassed to be talking about his own playing in front of these guys, but he also wanted desperately to keep the conversation going.

"I, uh . . . Yeah, I was named first flautist in the Pennsylvania All-State Band."

"No kidding!" Jermaine was impressed.

"You didn't tell me that!" James said jokingly to Henry.

For a moment Henry was speechless. He had so many questions that he didn't know where to begin.

"How does it feel when you improvise like that?" he asked Jermaine.

"Like heaven."

"Funny," Henry said.

"What's that?"

"That's what it's like listening to it too."

By this time, Henry was quickly becoming the band's mascot. When they began their next set, he stood by the saxophones for a while, then moved next to the upright bass. To be in the presence of music and musicians this good was like magic—the kind he wanted to learn how to create himself, over and over again.

Just like seeing *The Crusades* on the big screen, the day on the boat completely rearranged Henry's brain musically. He joined another group, the Beaver Territory Band, and was anxious to start working out some of the things he'd learned listening to the group on the boat. He got his chance when a new trumpet player showed up to sub for the regular guy. The trumpet sub was named Roy, a sixteen-year-old black kid whose sophistication was exactly what Henry was thirsting for. From the moment Roy blew his first note, Henry knew there was a lot he could learn from him. As the band ran through several of their tunes, Roy took things to a whole new level. When the leader called for a five, Henry went over to introduce himself.

"Hi, I'm Henry," he said.

"Oh, I'm Roy. Good to meet you, Henry."

"Say, where'd you learn to play like that?"

Roy laughed. "Oh, man, I don't know. Listening, mostly."

"You've never taken lessons?"

"Just from my uncle. He plays in a big band and gave me this trumpet when he got a new one."

"So, you learn mostly by ear? Whatta you have, perfect pitch or something?"

Roy shrugged. "I never thought about it."

Henry just stared back at Roy in amazement.

"Hey, has anyone showed you the 6/9 chord yet? You know, the one that Duke is using a lot?" Roy said.

"6/9 chord? No. What is it?" Henry asked.

Roy proceeded to demonstrate. The wheels in Henry's brain started spinning fast as he quickly tried to integrate this new information.

After rehearsal, he rushed home and stayed up all night exploring the 6/9, playing it chromatically up and down. He wanted to hear how the lush and beautiful chord sounded in every key. Roy had sent him on a totally new trajectory, opening an exciting new door. Coming into contact with more black musicians expanded Henry's awareness not just in music—which was deepening his appreciation of the influence of black music and musicians on American popular music—but it also increased his sensitivity to the role of race in society in general. There were only a few black students at Aliquippa High School and Henry began to think more about what life must be like for them. One event in particular had shaken him to the core.

After attending a meeting with Jack on how to be a good citizen at the Hi-Y club, a branch of the YMCA for high school boys, a group began walking home together. The message of the meeting must have not made much impact, because a few of the boys started throwing rocks at streetlamps. Dozens of stones were hurled into the dark night sky until one finally hit the light, shattering it completely.

"Oh, man! We got it!" one of the boys said.

"Who threw that winner?" another asked.

"Henry, was that you?" Jack wanted to know.

"I didn't throw any. But, man, what a *beautiful* sound it made . . ." he said kind of dreamily.

The other boys were not sure what to make of this response.

A few minutes later, a police car turned the corner. As it approached, officers focused a light on the broken glass on the street and then, like a spotlight, over to the boys. Henry pulled down his fedora and broke off from the group as the police stopped to question them.

"Say, boys, you know anything about this smashed-out light?"

They froze with fear as the officers stared them down. Then one spoke. "Just what a beautiful sound it made when it broke?"

The two officers exchanged a look.

"All right, wise guys, get in the squad car. You can explain all this to your parents when they pick you up at the station."

As the police car passed Henry further down the street, he tipped his hat to Jack and flashed him a sly smile. He let out a little laugh, tickled that he was able to gracefully duck getting in any kind of trouble. The big smile remained until he reached the end of the block. Then it vanished in an instant. Across the way, he saw crosses burning on the hillside and it stopped him cold. He gasped audibly. He thought of his new friend Roy and it made him upset and angry to think of Roy ever having to see anything like this that signaled the horrible hate some people carried in their hearts. It terrified Henry that these kinds of people were in the world, much less in his own town. If there were one thing he'd learned in all his years of going to church, it was that God created man in his own image. Nothing about the way these people thought made any sense to Henry and he prayed Roy would never come across anything like this. He tried to calm himself by believing that God would protect Roy.

The more Henry was learning outside the Aliquippa High School band, the more he ended up clashing with the band director, who had one way of running things and didn't tolerate suggestions or insights from students. When Henry turned sixteen, Aliquippa made it into the all-state band competition in Punxsutawney, Pennsylvania, the home of the famous groundhog. Henry was disappointed but not entirely surprised when the band director only chose one student to play a solo, and it was Jack. Henry felt that his not being chosen was supposed to serve as some kind of punishment, but he was also genuinely happy for Jack. He knew how hard his friend worked and admired his diligence in practicing his trumpet every day.

When competition day arrived and they boarded the band bus for Punxsutawney, the entire band was very hyped up and Jack was beginning to feel the pressure. There were dozens of bands from all over the state—nothing but top high school musicians as far as the eye could see and the ear could hear. The Aliquippa Quips sat in their designated area, feeling more intimidated by the level of musicianship around them with each passing minute. Some kids started to break out in a sweat. Had they practiced enough? Why did some of the bands sound so *professional*?

Finally, the time arrived for them to take to the field to perform. The piece got off to a strong start and the band members found their confidence. Then it came time for Jack's solo and Henry watched his friend with pride. Everything sounded great until the end of the section, where Jack missed his high C note. His face turned tomato red and Henry felt terrible! He could see how upset Jack was. The Quips had now lost any chance they had at taking home a trophy and that would forever be blamed on Jack. Knowing Jack better than anyone, Henry knew there was only one thing to do now—make him laugh. But how?

As the band marched off the field and into the locker room, Jack did not want to face the wrath of the band director and rushed over to Henry.

"I need to find a men's room. NOW," Jack demanded.

Henry took his meaning—Jack just needed to disappear for a moment. Scanning the area quickly, Henry spotted just the place and ushered his friend in that direction. As they ducked inside, Jack spotted a trashcan and dropped his horn squarely inside it. Henry very calmly reached in and began pulling out used towels and trash before rescuing his friend's trumpet from the unknown gunk and grime.

"Oh, man, I blew it. I mean, I really *blew it*," Jack said.

Henry swatted this idea away with a flick of his wrist. "Nah," he said. Then he took a moment to set up his perfect timing. "But you know what I did notice?"

"What's that?" Jack asked.

"When you blew that note, I think I saw Punxsutawney Phil pop out of his hole with both ears covered!"

Jack erupted with such a howl that Henry had to drop his mock seriousness immediately and join in the laughter.

"That'll teach band director McCullough not to pick anyone for a solo except Henry Mancini from now on!" Jack said.

"Well, if it'll make you feel any better, you can come over to my house and I can ask my father to whack your knuckles."

They walked out of the boys' room arm in arm, friends for life.

One of the few perks of living in Aliquippa was that there was a little bit of money to be made as a young musician. With nearly every European ethnicity in the area, one could be hired to play all the weddings and get paid all-you-can-eat plus maybe an actual dollar or two. Aliquippa was a prearranged town split into "Plans" designated by Jones and Laughlin Steel after their purchase of the town, which was on the ruins of an old amusement park. The company divided the area for its workers into a dozen different sections that segregated people by ethnicity. Italians, Serbs, Croats, Irish, Poles, and others were all placed strictly according to their race. For example, Plan 6 was for management and Plan 11 extension was for black people who had come north during the Great Migration.

One Saturday, while Henry was getting ready for the wedding of a Czech friend of his father's from work, Quinto came into his room. He sat down on Henry's bed while holding all of Henry's handwritten Artie Shaw arrangements.

"Son," he said.

"Yes, Father?"

"It is good—all this experience on the bandstand that you are getting from playing weddings."

"And don't forget the cake."

"Yes," Quinto said. "But because you will go to college to become a music teacher, you will need to learn more about arranging. You already have a good basic understanding, which I can see from all the work you do. But what if you are not doing it right? You need someone to show you. You don't want to learn things wrong. That will only make them harder to learn correctly."

"Who could teach me?" Henry asked.

"I was wondering the same thing. So, I asked your piano teacher and he told me there is someone right across the street from him in Pittsburgh—a man who is a conductor and arranger at the Stanley Theatre. His name is Max something. We will go to meet him this week after your piano lesson."

The following Saturday, they entered through the stage door of the Stanley Theatre as Henry's music teacher had instructed them. Searching the hallway, Henry spotted Max Adkins' name on one of the doors. Quinto knocked and the door opened, revealing a dapper gentleman on the other side.

"Mr. Mancini? Henry? I've been expecting you. Please, sit down."

"Thank you," Quinto said.

"Mr. Ochsenhardt tells me that you are becoming an excellent piano player, Henry."

Before Henry could say anything, Quinto interjected. "He listens to the radio nonstop, always writing all these notes on paper. He needs someone to teach him."

"Well, that's very exciting, Henry. You would like to learn arranging?" Max asked Henry.

"Oh, yes. I mean, I've been trying to teach myself what I can from writing out all the Artie Shaw charts," Henry said, pulling out a stack of his collection of copied arrangements and handing them to Max.

Astonished, Max thumbed through them quickly and looked up at Henry. "You even made your own music paper?"

Henry stared back with his trademark naïveté. "Don't you?"

Max smiled broadly. "You've come to the right place, Henry. I'd be happy to teach you everything I know. And maybe you could teach me a thing or two."

A few weeks into his studies, Henry found out that Max didn't teach just high school students—he'd taught Billy Strayhorn, who Henry knew had just gone off with Duke Ellington's band. The idea that Max taught Billy and was now teaching Henry brought an actual tingling into his fingers. He wanted to impress Max and show him how much he could learn and how hard he was willing to work. And then there was the fact that Max was one of the few people at the time who actually had a system for teaching arranging. Stock arrangements put out by music publishers were designed for a set number of players—say fifteen, ten, or five—so it was the job of the arranger to create flexibility in the charts. Max's method was to give Henry the parts of a stock arrangement for the individual instruments and have him reconstruct the full score from that. Through this exercise, Henry came to learn what was essential and what was expendable. It required creative thinking and challenged his musical mind like never before.

The other amazing thing about being Max's student was that because he was the resident arranger and conductor at the Stanley Theatre, he invited Henry to listen to all the bands that would come to play there. Not only was this thrilling, but it also allowed him to synthesize everything he was learning in his lessons with Max. Henry's aptitude for orchestration was developing simultaneously alongside his natural knack for understanding and writing melodies. Max couldn't help but be incredibly impressed with his new young student. Something told him that Henry could go far. To prepare him for everything else that would come with the territory, Max turned to Henry one day after his lesson.

"I've got half an hour before rehearsal. What do you say we take a walk and I'll introduce you to my tailor, Mr. Bellantoni. Every musician needs at least one good suit. Your father will be pleased he is Italian."

"Sure. Thank you, Max. How will I pay for the suit, though?"

"I will have you do some copy work for me. This is very important, Henry. Very important, indeed."

On another occasion, Max took Henry out to a diner to do some work. It was the first time Max asked for Henry's help on the arrangements for an act that was coming to the Stanley. When their bill arrived, Max took it as he reached into his pocket for his money clip. Then he placed it down in front of Henry.

"See the total amount there?"

"Yes," Henry replied.

"That's not actually the total."

"It's not?"

"Whenever someone gives you service and waits on you, you must give them a tip. Folks in the service industry rely on tips to make a living. As musicians, we're in a unique place to understand this."

"We are?"

"Sure," Max said. "Leaving a good tip is also good for us. When we're good to others who work hard, people will take care of us when we work hard. Your father, he makes a salary at the mill. That means he can rely on being paid the same amount of money each week. But when you're a waitress or a musician, you don't always know how much you'll make in a week or a month. So, if you're generous with others, chances are, people will be generous with you."

Henry thought about this for a while, then said, "You know, Max, that makes a lot of sense."

Max was an incredible mentor to Henry, who was very eager to learn everything he could about music and life. The more training Henry got for arranging, the more excited he got about music in general. He started to believe that he could really have a future in it, just like Max. He got so wrapped up in his arranging assignments that he brought them to school each day and became very skilled at slipping them under his schoolwork when the teacher would come by to commend his diligent study habits. On the day Max took Henry to be fitted by Mr. Bellantoni, he told Henry about an idea that had occurred to him.

"So, I've been thinking, Henry. You really should apply to Juilliard," Max said.

"The Juilliard in New York?"

"You know of it?"

"Of course. But I don't know if my father would be able to pay for a private conservatory like Juilliard," Henry said.

"I don't think he would have to pay very much, because you would receive a scholarship."

"You really think so?"

"Well, we'll never know if you don't audition."

"And wearing this suit," Mr. Bellantoni chimed in, "how could you lose?"

The only real downside to studying with Max Adkins was that it caused Henry to quickly outgrow his high school band director as well as his music theory teacher. The tensions between Henry and the director came to such a head that Henry was kicked out of band in his senior year. That meant that the only time Henry and Jack would see each other in school was if they took music theory together, even though the teacher had a reputation for being the strictest of sticklers. For the class's final exam, the students were asked to apply all the rules of theory to harmonize the song "America." Instead, Henry made up his own rules; the teacher took one glance at his test and threw it in the trash. Somehow, Henry was still able to graduate. It was 1942 and he was only eighteen.

Then, days after graduation, the King of Swing himself arrived at the Stanley Theatre with his big band for a week-long engagement. Max took Henry by surprise when he called him down the hall to Benny Goodman's dressing room. Henry pointed and mouthed to Max, *Is he in there?*

Max smiled and raised his eyebrows, cool cat that he was.

Henry reached the doorway to Benny's dressing room and stood next to Max.

"Benny, this is the kid I was telling you about," Max said. "I really think he should do an arrangement for you."

Henry stuck out his hand to shake with Benny Goodman. "It's an honor to meet you, Mr. Goodman."

"Henry is on his way to New York to audition for Juilliard, so he will be there during your week at the Paramount," Max told Benny.

"Great. Drop in and see me there, kid. I'll find an assignment for you," Benny said. "If you're as good as Max here says, there could be even more work for you."

Chapter Three

NEW IN NEW YORK

A few days before Henry's Juilliard audition, he went to meet Benny Goodman at the Paramount as planned. Goodman was strictly business.

"Hey, kid. You made it."

He shuffled through a pile of music on a table, searching.

"I was thinking you could take a crack at this one?" Benny said, holding up a piece entitled "Idaho."

"Oh, I love this tune," Henry said.

"Great. There's a piano up in the attic where you can work."

"Thank you, Mr. Goodman. Thank you very much," Henry said, backing up before spinning on his heel to run off to work.

Henry found the attic and holed up there, working feverishly on the arrangement. "Idaho" was a fox-trot that had charted in the Top 5 that year. There was a lot to work with and Henry knew it was his big chance to impress *the* Benny Goodman. He wasn't being paid, but that wasn't going to stop him from sequestering himself for hours on end without even taking time to eat.

A few times a day, the only break he would allow himself was to practice the Beethoven sonata he'd prepared for his Juilliard audition. Feeling pretty good about that, he'd jump right back on "Idaho," much more excited about writing for Goodman and his legendary brass section. Finally, he emerged with his finished work and handed Benny enough copies for all the members of the band while the musicians were on a five.

"All right," Benny said, looking it over. "We'll run it through once everyone's back."

Henry did his best to control the butterflies in his stomach. He took a seat in the theater and watched the band shuffle back on stage. Benny had already begun placing copies of Henry's arrangement on each player's music stand. As soon as everyone was settled in, Benny called the tune and the musicians brought their instruments to the ready position. It all started out just fine, but Henry quickly realized he'd written way too high, having been overly excited about the great brass section. This was considered a major rookie mistake—in addition to how incredibly challenging the arrangement was, which can showcase your chops as an arranger but doesn't make you any friends in the band. Benny raised a fist in the air, the signal for the band to stop. Then he turned to look at Henry, the only person in the audience.

"Well, kid, I don't think you're ready."

Henry walked out of the Paramount into a biting wind, feeling a bag of mixed emotions—how could he have let himself get so carried away? Why did he have to get so ambitious anyway? Max had taught him how to excel, how to do his most creative work, and how to stand out. Oh, he was standing out all right! This latest lesson was one Max hadn't taught him and one he had to learn the hard way—an arranger needs to put himself in the shoes of the musicians who have lots of other songs to get through—some with already tough enough arrangements. Henry knew he would have to find a way to make whatever group he was writing for sound great without killing them in the process.

Rattled by the experience and wishing he could somehow go back in time just this once, he felt some of the wind seep out of his sails going into his Juilliard audition. He'd practiced his piece for weeks and may have known it better than Beethoven ever did at this point. Now all he needed to do was shake off what happened and not blow his next great opportunity. Things moved fast in New York!

On the morning of his audition, Henry rose early and dressed in the sharp suit tailor-made by Mr. Bellantoni. He decided to follow another piece of advice from Max—get a shoeshine before the audition so he would look his best from head to toe. It also gave him a chance to go over the sonata a few more times in his head. He just wished he didn't feel that his entire future hinged on this moment. It was an enormous pressure he'd never felt before. As he stepped into the seat for a shoeshine, he once again began running through the music in his mind, and he began to doubt whether he and Max had chosen the right piece. Was it challenging enough? He tipped generously, just as Max had always urged him to do, and began walking uptown on Broadway until he reached Sixty-Fifth Street. When he saw the sign outside the storied conservatory, he took in as much air into his lungs as he could and let it escape slowly. No turning back now.

He entered the room, where the buttoned-up evaluators and the dean sat stoically. It was clear they wanted him to get right to it, as one of them gestured toward the piano. Henry had to admit, the suit did make him feel self-assured as he felt all eyes follow him across the room. He pulled out the bench, sat down, and hovered his hands over the piano keys momentarily. Then he began. He felt confident playing—he figured he would always be more comfortable with music as his first language over anything else. As soon as he finished, he knew he had executed it perfectly. It was now literally and figuratively out of his hands, and an enormous sense of relief came over him, even as the judges began whispering.

One of them looked up at Henry with a question. "Is there something else you can play for us?"

Henry was not expecting this! He had to think fast on his feet. For some reason, his mind bounced back to the time he had to figure out how to make Jack laugh after blowing that note at the All-State competition. Suddenly, without a hint of doubt in his voice, he answered.

"I recently wrote a fantasy on Cole Porter's 'Night and Day.' Would that be all right?"

"Yes, please. Go ahead, Mr. Mancini."

What followed was a stunning and brilliant rendering of the tune, with every scale, flourish, and run Henry could think of. It was five minutes of pure musical genius filled with wonderful grace notes—those non-essential but inspired additions.

"Oh, that's marvelous," one of the audition panelists said.

Not even the experts at Juilliard could tell that what they'd just heard was purely improvised. If they had known, they only would have been even more impressed—but this fact was going to remain Henry's little secret.

"Welcome to Juilliard," they said.

Henry felt himself practically float out the front doors of the building. He wandered around in a daze, just thinking about all the world-class musicians who'd played in the places he was now walking past on a daily basis, from Carnegie Hall to Radio City. His acceptance into Juilliard was already working to soften the blow from the Benny Goodman debacle. With a newfound spring in his step, he glided down Columbus Avenue, feeling extra proud of his Italian heritage.

In a phone booth in midtown, he rang Max to share the news.

"I got in, Max! I played the sonata and then they asked if I had anything else, and the first thing that came to mind was 'Night and Day,' so I went with that and just played the heck out of it."

"Congratulations, Henry! I knew you could do it."

"But, Max—I blew it with Benny Goodman. I mean, really blew it! I feel terrible after you recommended me. I know it can't reflect well on you and I'm really sorry."

"Listen here, there's no need for apology. You learned a valuable lesson, did you not?" Max said.

"Valuable? More like priceless."

"Well, that's good to hear, because I just recommended you for another gig."

"You really are a glutton for punishment!"

"No, Henry! Just because you have tremendous talent doesn't mean you still don't have a whole lot to learn about working in the real world."

"So, what's the job?" Henry asked.

"There's a daily noontime radio show hosted by this Portuguese cat named Vincent Lopez. I thought you might be jazzed to know that one of his previous sidemen was your favorite, Artie Shaw. It's broadcasted from the Roseland Ballroom on West Fifty-Second Street. Do you know where that is?"

Suddenly, Henry was speechless.

"Henry? Henry, are you still there?"

"Yes, I'm here. Sorry. It's just, you're not going to believe this, but . . ."

"What?"

"I'm standing right across from it."

Henry returned to the Roseland the following day for the job, which turned out to be as a secondary piano player for the bandleader and pianist Lopez. When he walked in, a producer rushed over, handed him a stack of charts, and directed him to a piano. Being that it was radio, none of Lopez's listeners were aware that this secondary person even existed. Lopez began the show the way he did every time, with the sign-on:

"Hello, everybody—Lopez speaking," which would later become the most enduring of any major American bandleader's signatures. The theme song of the show was "Nola," a novelty ragtime piece from 1915. Lopez had a flamboyant piano-playing style, which later was said to have influenced Liberace. Lopez was a showman to his core and had no intention of sharing the spotlight unless it served him. Maybe it was his newfound self-confidence from his Juilliard acceptance and the discovery of his improvisational skills, but Henry got carried away instead of simply supporting the star of the show. This was his second rookie mistake—playing too loud and too much, and completely overshadowing Lopez. As soon as the show was over, Vincent marched over to him.

"What the hell do you think you're doing, whippersnapper? Whose show do you think this is, anyway?"

"Uh . . ." Henry was at a loss for words, thinking that if he was hired to play piano, he should play his best.

"What's your name?"

"Henry Mancini."

"All right, Henry. You're fired!"

Henry was crestfallen. "Sir, if you give me another shot, I can play whatever you want."

"Get out! *Vá com Deus*!"

That meant *Go with God* in Portuguese, although to Henry it didn't sound all that sincere.

It wasn't until classes began a couple of weeks later that Henry's real frustration began. Juilliard was an extremely strict, conservatory environment, which did not allow Henry to take any arranging classes his first year—the thing he was most interested in. Juilliard hadn't caught up with the times just yet, so Henry was forced into being a piano major, and that meant that there many prerequisite courses to get out of the way first. Henry found this suffocating to his creative energies after having become accustomed to Max's nurturing and personalized teaching style.

This reality was only made worse by being a broke student in New York City. The only money he had was whatever his father could afford to send; by the end of each month, Henry was making three Hershey bars into his three meals of the day. But just when he was finding himself more and more down each day, he discovered the listening room on campus. This was where he could check out any record album he liked and spend countless hours listening to Ravel, Debussy, Tchaikovsky, and dozens of others as he followed along with the written scores. He made his way through all the other composers one by one and fully immersed himself in their works. He said many years later that this served him well all throughout his career and was the best use of his time at Juilliard.

By the second semester of freshman year, Henry was becoming known as "Hank" to most of his friends and classmates. On his eighteenth birthday, he went to register for the draft and was shortly thereafter sent for basic training in Atlantic City, a hotbed for musicians hoping to join the Army Air Corps Band that big bandleader Glenn Miller was putting together. All the musicians would gather at the rathskeller in the Knights of Columbus Hotel in Atlantic City with the hopes of getting assigned to Miller's band, which would be stationed at Yale before shipping out overseas. Lots of the guys encouraged Hank to go see Miller, which Hank felt pretty intimidated about doing. Finally, he worked up the courage and went to meet him in his office.

Hank entered with a salute to Miller, who stared back blankly at him over rimless glasses.

"I hear you're an arranger. Do you write well? Are you a good writer?"

All Hank could manage was, "Well enough for what I've done, I suppose."

Hank could only hope that Miller hadn't heard about the disaster with Benny Goodman.

"I also play flute, piccolo, and piano."

"Write down your name and serial number here," Miller said.

Hank did as he was asked.

"You're dismissed, Airman."

Hank saluted again and walked out, not sure what to make of what just happened.

As it turned out, Miller did not take Hank into his own band, but he *did* recommend him for the Twenty-Eighth Army

Air Corps Band. This was extremely fortunate for Hank, as the alternative would have been gunnery school. Without Glenn Miller, Hank may have never survived the war. He called his old friend Jack from a payphone in New Jersey.

"I can't be too disappointed about not making it into Glenn Miller's band," Hank told his pal.

"Hey, he thought you were good enough to recommend you for another band. Anything's better than gunnery school," Jack said. "You know what they say about that."

"No, what's that?"

"That the life expectancy of a tail gunner in combat is measured not in minutes, but in seconds."

"Well, sure, when you put it that way!"

Hank remained in Atlantic City for less than a year before being stationed to Seymour Johnson Air Force Base in North Carolina, which, he told his parents, was truly awful. The only bright spot was when the movie star Tony Martin got assigned to sing in their band. From that point on, the 28th Band became the 528th Band, and went to Scott Field, Illinois, where Quinto and Anna visited.

When his mother saw her son in uniform for the first time, she began to cry—more out of pride than anything.

"You look so grown and so handsome," she told him in her strong Italian accent.

"I've missed you and Father," Henry said.

They walked to town and had an early dinner.

"It's too bad you had to leave school so soon," Anna said.

"Once the war is won, he will go back," Quinto assured her, without any input from Henry.

From December 1944 to January 1945, about nineteen thousand American soldiers were killed in what came to be known as the Battle of the Bulge, the last major German offensive of World War II and the bloodiest and most costly for American troops. The United States high command decided after this that Air Force musicians would make great infantry soldiers, so it was six weeks of infantry training for Hank before shipping off to Le Havre, France. He first heard the news of Roosevelt's death while standing on a French railway platform on April 12, 1945, wondering what fate lay before him.

Chapter Four

BEARING WITNESS

Like so many other young men sent off to fight in the war, Hank had no idea what to expect or what would become of him. All he had were his wits and the moral compass that had been forming within him for the first twenty years of his life. He was shipped off to Le Havre, which means "the harbor" in French, in the Normandy region of France where the Seine River meets the English Channel. Built on former marshland and mudflats that were drained in the sixteenth century, Le Havre is the second-largest port in France and in 1944 was the home to a combat engineers' brigade.

In the years prior to Hank's arrival, Le Havre's piers and lock gates had become severely eroded by the constantly changing tide. Reparations to the lock gates using new techniques in engineering made Le Havre useful to Allied vessels at all times of day regardless of the tide. Beginning in November 1944, Le Havre developed into the principal troop debarkation point in the European theater.

The company of engineers that Hank was assigned to included a chaplain in need of an organist. The chaplain commandeered Hank to drive his jeep and conduct services in the field with a pump organ, an ornately carved wood two-level organ that required no electricity because of its foot-operated pumps that pushed air in to carry the sound out. Shortly after Hank arrived, he was ordered by the chaplain to drive from the base in Le Havre to Épernay, east of Paris, about a three-and-a-half-hour drive. The chaplain was insufferable, treating Hank like his personal chauffeur. Once in Épernay, the chaplain began snapping up as many cases of champagne as he could get his hands on and barked at Hank and the others to load them into the jeep. Hank asked one of his comrades what on earth was going on.

"One person can't possibly drink this much, can they?"

"He buys it here on the cheap and then turns around to sell it at an outrageous markup to the soldiers."

"How can he get away with that? A man of the cloth, no less!"

"I guess you haven't heard the expression 'all is fair in love and war'?"

"Can't say that I have."

Hank shot a very angry look at the chaplain, who was leaning up against the side of a barn and leisurely smoking as Hank and the others worked up a sweat loading the jeep.

Hank had never been the kind of person who was known to speak ill of anyone, but in letters he wrote home he characterized the chaplain as "a crook and an absolutely dreadful human being." One day on the way back from a field service for several of the fallen, the chaplain ordered Hank to take a detour. They arrived in a small country village, where the chaplain began hollering orders for the men to remove stained glass from a damaged church. Hank guessed it had been there for centuries and considered this act to be absolute sacrilege.

"I have a hard time believing this has anything to do with our mission," Hank said to the chaplain.

"What do you know about our mission?"

"I know I've been assigned to play this awful pump organ that's not even in concert pitch. Not to help you enrich yourself through theft."

This looting of stained glass continued as they made their way around France. Apparently, many others had tried to rein in the chaplain through complaints up the chain of command, but nothing ever came of it—even when the chaplain asked the engineers to crate the stained glass and ship it back to the United States. Hank wondered if the engineers knew what he was up to or if they were also in on it. He was beginning to understand what was meant by "all is fair in love and war," although it didn't sit well with him at all.

Despite the terrible and downright criminal behavior he witnessed on the part of the chaplain, nothing could have ever prepared Hank for May 5, 1945. On this day, Hank's unit was sent into the Mauthausen concentration camp in Austria—the last of the camps to be liberated. Along with Allied units, they were there to free about forty thousand prisoners from Mauthausen and nearby Gusen. Just days before, the majority of the SS had fled once they'd become aware of the approaching Allies. As Hank's unit entered the camp, the first thing he noticed were two tall smokestacks sticking out of the building that housed the gas chamber. As they drove down the main road of the camp, they saw prisoners in stripes wandering around with rifles and guarding the last few SS men. Others were busy burying the dead, as hundreds of prisoners had died just days before their arrival and many more perished in the days after—they were so weak and beyond the help of medical aid from US military forces.

Hank couldn't help but find it strange how bright of a day it was. It made him think of another expression he'd learned recently attributed to the Supreme Court Justice Louis Brandeis: "Sunlight is the best disinfectant." The camp seemed to be encapsulated in a giant cloud of dust, which Hank thought must have been due to the rock quarry. There wasn't a tree or plant in sight, and it reminded Hank of photos he'd seen of the Dust Bowl in America a decade before. It was horrific and he knew he wanted to quickly get everyone as far away from there as possible.

Hank and his comrades were shown "the stairs of death," which were situated at the base of the camp's quarry. Prisoners were forced to carry rocks—some that weighed over one hundred pounds—up 186 stairs, which often caused them to lose their balance, fall, and create a domino effect, knocking everyone else down to their deaths. Hank wondered what had to happen to people to allow them to dream up such acts of barbarism and cruelty. Mauthausen was classified as a Grade III camp, one of the toughest where this kind of hard labor was reserved specifically for the extermination of the intelligentsia, who were considered the Reich's most powerful political enemies. It seemed that the oppressive sun burning down that day was needed to melt the cloud of evil hanging over the place. Hank was never the same after bearing witness to the total absence of humanity and recoiled as he stood beside incinerators that were still warm to the touch.

Three days later, on May 8, 1945, Charles de Gaulle

announced the French people's freedom and the end of World War II in Europe, proclaiming it Victory Day. Hank heard about church bells ringing out across France to spread this message that the six-year war and Nazi oppression was over. Just as he was getting caught up in the thoughts of peace and revelry in the streets of France, a rumor began circulating that his unit was going to be reassigned to the Pacific Theater to fight the Japanese. As they were preparing to leave the horrors of Mauthausen behind them forever, he was called aside by his commanding officer.

"Hank. It seems the gods are smiling down on you."

"How do you mean, sir?"

"Better get that flute of yours all shined up. Hope you won't miss that pump organ too much."

Hank shot him a look—it was widely known how much Hank hated that thing, even though it had more to do with the chaplain than anything else.

"So, I'll be in another band?" Hank asked, halfway happy about the news.

"An infantry band," the officer said. "You ever heard of the French Riviera?"

Hank's mouth dropped. "You're not toying with me, are you?"

"Ha! No, I just wish I were going with you. You're going straight from hell to paradise, friend!"

Hank arrived in Nice, where he checked into the Ruhl Hotel on the Promenade des Anglais, the coastal walkway built by the English aristocracy in the eighteenth century, when they began wintering there. Hank breathed in the salty air of the Mediterranean, feeling lucky to be alive and fortunate to be where he was. The first Frenchman he met outside of the American Red Cross Casino approached him with a smile and a handshake.

"You must be having the very best luck to just arrive here in Nice now," the young Frenchman said to him.

"This is the most beautiful place I could ever imagine," Hank said in a dreamy voice.

"The very name Nice came from the Greek *Nikaia*, which means City of Victory. And it is here that you are celebrating the victory!" The Frenchman grabbed Hank's arm, raising it in the air like a boxer who'd won his match.

"*Liberté*!" Hank said.

The place was absolutely jubilant. Every man, woman, and child was out celebrating and rejoicing as champagne flowed in the streets. Royal blue beach umbrellas lined the sand as far as the eye could see. Hank met up with a few of his buddies and together they proceeded to promenade along the shore, turning the heads of some radiant Frenchwomen embodying joie de vivre once again in a country of peace. Hank and his friends found a place to rent pedal boats and pedaled along the shore, where they came across some of the more obvious remnants of the war—a Nazi administration office, barricaded buildings, and scrap metal on the beach left over from the landmark Casino de la Jettée, which had been salvaged to build Nazi aircraft.

Hank's favorite cousin, Helen, who lived back in the States, had a husband named Ralph, who had been working behind German lines in the north of Italy. Hank's mother had written to Ralph asking him to help her track down her Henry. For Ralph, who served in the Army's Counter Intelligence Corps, it wasn't too hard to locate Hank in Nice. Nearing the end of the summer in 1945, Ralph contacted Hank's commanding officer to ask permission for Hank and a few friends to take leave for a couple of days. A message was sent to Hank to inform him where to meet Ralph in two days' time.

Hank was standing on a corner in Nice with his Italian-American buddies when Ralph showed up in a convertible Alfa Romeo.

"You'll never guess whose car this is," Ralph said as pulled up. "Or *was* . . ."

Hank reached over the door to shake hands with Ralph. "Good to see you, cousin. You didn't have to steal a car to come get us, though," Hank joked.

Ralph continued, "Not stolen—more like liberated. It belonged to one Clara Petacci."

One of Hank's buddies said, "Mussolini's mistress?"

"Bingo!"

"She was captured along with him, wasn't she?"

"Shot and then strung up alongside him over a petrol station in Milan."

To drive out the grisly thought, Hank said, "I guess you should always choose your lovers carefully."

"George here doesn't do that!" one of them said teasingly.

They all laughed.

"Now, you boys ready for some fun?" Ralph asked, revving up the engine.

They drove along the curvy coastline of the Côte d'Azur, stopping at beach after beautiful beach. At one point, one of Hank's friends told Ralph, "Hey, you know this guy's gonna be a big star, right?"

"Is that so?" Ralph asked.

"Sure is. You wanna put some money on it?" the friend said, smiling at Hank.

Those few days of leave spent at a villa Ralph had arranged for them to stay in were Hank's first chance to begin shaking off some of the war's horrors. Hank loved every little thing about Nice and never wanted to leave. He was getting paid to play music in the most gorgeous place on earth with the best food and a culture he was beginning to adopt as his own.

But before he could get too accustomed to this life, March of 1946 brought with it repatriation efforts and Hank was sent back to Fort Dix, New Jersey. On his first day back, he ran into his former Master Sergeant, Norman Leyden.

"Hank, is that you? Good to see you stateside and all in one piece."

"Same to you, Norman. What are you up to these days?" Hank asked.

"I'm chief arranger for the Glenn Miller Band."

Henry's face dropped. "But I thought . . ."

"Yes, Glenn's plane disappeared over the Channel last year. His widow, Helen, now owns the postwar civilian Miller band."

Then, without missing a beat, he added, "We sure could use a pianist."

Once again, Hank couldn't believe his luck.

He knew his father wouldn't be particularly happy about him not going back to Juilliard, but being offered a job as a professional musician was all Hank ever wanted. As the Gershwin tune went, "Nice work if you can get it." He could always go back to school later if he had to, but right now he felt he had to ride this train for as long as he could. But first, he had to ride the rails back home to see his parents.

~

Hank had gone away a boy and come back a man. His mother could see this in his eyes before taking him into her arms and squeezing him as hard as she could.

"God heard my prayers," she told him.

Hank was very grateful that his parents would no longer have to worry about him every minute of every day. Not everyone from his hometown was so lucky.

"Many of the men at the mill . . . their boys didn't come home," his father told him.

They sat in silence for a while before Hank went to the closet and pulled out the case that he'd first taken out all those years ago. He opened it, assembled the piccolo, and played his mother's favorite Italian folk song, "O Campagnola Bella." She began to cry tears of joy.

Before dinner, Hank went into town to meet some of his old high school friends who were survivors of the Sixty-Sixth Division from Aliquippa. They ordered a round of beers and talked about how strange it was to be home. Hank was horrified to hear what had happened to some of their classmates, bandmates, and friends from the Sixty-Sixth. His friend George began to fill him in.

"Some real bad weather closed in on them and the Germans started counterattacking until they had them completely surrounded near Bastogne in Belgium," George said. "They fought for days without any air support and were horribly defeated. Everyone and anyone who could hold a gun—cooks, clerks, and musicians—went on the line."

It was almost as though Hank knew what his friend was going to say next.

"The band . . . was completely *wiped out*."

Hank lowered his head, thinking about all these young men from his town whom he grew up with and were now gone just when their lives were supposed to be beginning. He realized that if he had been drafted from Aliquippa instead of New York, he probably wouldn't be sitting there at that moment. They ordered another round to toast these local heroes, the friends they would never see again.

He returned home to have dinner with his parents. His mother had made his favorite Italian dishes—*sagne e fagioli*, a noodle soup with peppers and pork, and *pecora al cotturo*, lamb stuffed with herbs.

"Perhaps you can even take classes this summer before returning to your studies in the fall?" his father asked.

Hank knew it wasn't going to be easy, but he had to tell his father that he'd made other plans. "The thing is . . ." he began, prompting a look of worry on his mother's face. "I already have a job."

"What does that have to do with you getting your degree? For becoming a teacher?"

"This is an opportunity I just can't pass up," Hank told them.

Anna did not want to spoil the happy homecoming. She employed a famous tactic of Italian mothers by distracting them with more food.

"Have some sausage," she told them.

But it seemed that Quinto was finished talking.

Hank helped his mother clear the dishes and clean the kitchen.

The next day he dressed in uniform and bid his parents farewell. He was going to Pittsburgh to see Max before heading back to New York. Stepping off the train, he walked along the

Allegheny River before turning up Seventh Street to the Stanley Theatre. A smile spread across his face as the music floated out through was the stage door, where he entered and found his way to the front of the house. There, Max was onstage conducting his twenty-five-piece orchestra. Taking a seat in the theater, he watched Max work. The band was hopping and it filled Hank with joy. Max turned around and saw Hank, and he lit up. He made his way over and gave his favorite student a great, big hug.

"And in uniform too? Looking sharp, Henry."

"You're not looking too bad yourself. Call me Hank!"

"Oh, I like that!"

They both laughed and then Hank took a more serious tone. "Max, thank you. I mean, how can I even *begin* to thank you?"

"Just do what you were put on this earth to do!"

As Hank got back on a train headed for New York, he was overcome with the feeling that he needed to make the most of every moment he had left on this earth and try to squeeze enough life into his own for all those from Aliquippa who weren't as fortunate as he was to make it out of the war alive.

Chapter Five

A MATCH MADE IN MUSIC

Tex Beneke, who had become the bandleader of the postwar Glenn Miller Band, had such complete trust in his chief arranger, Norman Leyden, that Hank wasn't even required to audition. Something about this tugged at Hank's heart, though—it wasn't all that long ago that Hank went to see Glenn Miller in Atlantic City in the hopes of being considered for the Army band Miller was putting together. Hank had always wished for a do-over for that day. If he had it to do again, he would have tried to come across slightly less awkward and would have thought beforehand about more things he could say so that the meeting wasn't so darn short. He just wished he hadn't been so green, as they say. A big part of him wished he could audition for Glenn because that would mean that he was still alive.

"How's $125 a week?" Norman asked Hank. "We usually play a whole week in one town so it's not a terrible touring schedule."

They were sitting in a diner in Midtown having coffee and pie.

"Are you kidding me? It sounds fantastic," Hank replied. "Thank you, Norman. I mean it."

"Hey, we're lucky to have you."

This was an exciting time. Hank could hardly believe his good fortune, getting into such a phenomenal band straight out of the service. The writing on the wall had not yet come into focus that the big band era was about to come to an end. So, for now, these young musicians—some of the best anywhere—were living the life, touring the country, and delivering the joy of their swinging big sound that brought much happiness to people everywhere. With the war over, there was a lot to celebrate and it felt like a great time to be alive. The Glenn Miller Band included a vocal group called the Crew Chiefs. Hank joining the band dovetailed with the Crew Chiefs making their way out to pursue other avenues. When they gave their notice, Tex had to immediately begin considering replacements. At sound check one day, Norman approached Hank about this latest development.

"The Crew Chiefs gave me their notice," he said.

Hank was really beginning to develop his trademark dry sense of humor. "Was it something I said?"

Norman laughed. "Oh, sure, it's you! Of course!"

They chuckled.

"Tex and I have another vocal group in mind."

"Oh? Who's that?" Hank asked.

"They're called the Mello-Larks. Have you heard of them?"

"Of course! I've seen the ads all over town. 'Sweet! Swingy! Swoonful! Swell!'"

This cracked Norman up. "Yup, that's them! Anyway, Tex

would like to audition them, so we'll need you to provide the accompaniment Friday before the show."

"Sounds good. I'm sure they're gonna work out great," Hank smiled. "I'll do my best not to scare them off."

The Mello-Larks originally formed when friends Tommy Hamm and Jack Biermann got together and asked Bob Smith and a female singer, Lee Stayner, to join them. They were a great blend of voices, but it didn't last long—when Lee's husband returned from the war, the two of them moved away. So, it wasn't until the three guys found a fantastic sight-reading singer named Ginny O'Connor to join them in 1946 that they really began to take off. It was as though Ginny was a good luck charm, because shortly after she came aboard, they were invited to audition for the Glenn Miller Band. Ginny had been one of Mel Tormé's background singers, a group known as the Mel-Tones, before Mel decided to go out on his own.

Hank arrived at the Million Dollar Theatre in downtown Los Angeles to meet the piano tuner early in the afternoon the day of the auditions. A while later, Tex arrived. He always seemed so pleased to have Hank onboard, as he was the ultimate professional and seemed to elevate everything. Norman walked in and got set up.

"Good day, gentlemen. They should be here any minute. I'd like to hear them separately first before harmonies," Tex said.

"You got it, boss," Norman replied.

As they began chitchatting and joking about something or other, the door opened and in walked Ginny O'Connor.

"Oh, hello! I'm Ginny! The boys are just parking the car," she said, walking over to shake hands with each of them. When she approached Hank, who was sitting at the piano, she shook his hand a bit longer than she did with the other two. Hank felt his own hand pull away perhaps before Ginny's was ready to. Something electric passed between them, though if you'd asked Hank about it at that moment he probably would have just chalked it up to static electricity. But Ginny recognized it as something else right away. Hank was highly inexperienced in the romance department and hadn't even had a girlfriend in high school, so he was still fairly oblivious that he could have such an effect on a woman. Norman came over with some sheet music and handed it to Ginny.

"Word on the street is that you are one hell of a sight reader," Norman said.

"Learned it from my mama," she smiled.

"Ready to get started?"

"Without the boys?" Ginny asked.

"We want to hear each of you individually first. So, we'll start with you."

"Great!"

Norman told Hank which song to start with and Ginny took her place beside the piano. She wouldn't allow herself to look too long at the tall, cute Italian pianist for fear that it might break her concentration.

Hank looked up at her and said, "All set?"

She smiled, nodded, and hoped she wasn't blushing too much.

As he began to play she came in right on cue, singing while sight-reading an arrangement she'd never seen before. It was no joke—this gal knew her stuff. And her voice was downright heavenly. The rest of the Mello-Larks walked in while Ginny was still in the middle of the song. There was a heartfelt round of applause when she finished. The guys introduced themselves around and took turns singing individual parts before sealing the deal with their gorgeous harmonies.

Tex looked up with a giant grin. "Can you start rehearsing tomorrow?"

"YES!" Ginny answered the loudest.

As she and the Mello-Larks walked out of the audition, they jumped up and down in celebration.

"Ginny strikes again!" one of the guys exclaimed.

She laughed.

"*A prima vista*," she said, referencing the musical term for sight-reading, which literally means *at first sight*. What they didn't catch was the double entendre she intended to express how she felt seeing that pianist for the first time.

The feeling was not exactly the same for Hank. In addition to his inexperience, he was privately intimidated by Ginny, who was from Los Angeles and was therefore what he'd call one of those *Hollywood people*. He would tell his bandmates that he had lots of fun winking at girls from the bandstand only to find them waiting for him after the show. But the gentleman Hank was only twenty-three years old and had his mind primarily on music. When they began rehearsing, Ginny approached him all smiles—only to have Hank retreat behind the piano each time. He didn't like that he had to stay back and rehearse Ginny and the other singers sometimes while the rest of the band was out playing a round of golf. She only flirted innocently whenever she had the chance, but Hank wasn't playing along. This was unfortunate because what Ginny didn't know was that Hank seemed to have inherited his father's inability to express feelings, and perhaps even an inability to recognize them. But bassist Rolly Bundock saw that there could be something very special brewing between Ginny and the shy piano player. When she was feeling defeated one night after they'd already played a couple weeks of shows and she couldn't get Hank to say more than a few words to her, Rolly encouraged Ginny not too give up on Hank too soon.

On one of their long train rides from Los Angeles to New York City, Hank finally worked up the courage to sit next to Ginny.

"Is this seat taken?" he asked.

Ginny tried to contain her excitement. "No!" she said excitedly. Then she turned to look out the train car window, doing her best to come across as just slightly aloof before realizing that it was an exercise in futility—she couldn't help wanting to look right at him.

"So, uh . . ." Hank began. "Norman's got me doing some arranging for the band now."

"Oh, that's wonderful!"

Hank looked at her slightly sideways. Did everything that came out of her mouth always sound so chipper?

"Yes. So, I was wondering if there was anything in particular you would like to sing?"

"Well, yes, actually. There's a song coming out any day now called "The Christmas Song." One of my friends from Los Angeles, Nat King Cole, recorded it. And Mel Tormé, whom I used to sing with, as you know, co-wrote it with Bob Wells. And do you want to hear something amusing?"

"Sure," Hank said, doing his best to match her energy level.

"They wrote it on a sweltering August day just trying to keep cool! With lyrics like, 'Chestnuts roasting on an open fire, Jack Frost nipping at your nose' . . . Isn't that just a hoot?"

"It really is," Hank said with a laugh, which was probably

the first truly authentic response he'd given Ginny thus far. "Can you sing me a bit of the melody? I'll ask Norman to get a copy tomorrow."

Ginny sat up straight and cleared her throat. She hummed what she could remember and sang some of the lyrics while staring deeply into Hank's eyes. Very suddenly, he could feel himself getting into the Christmas spirit.

The following week, Hank wrote a gorgeous arrangement of "The Christmas Song." Tex rehearsed it with the band and it was a stunner. It would be a perfect addition to their holiday set. When they arrived in New York in early December, Nat King Cole's instant classic had not yet been released. At their show at the 400 Club, they were shocked and delighted when Nat King Cole, Mel Tormé, and a handful of other celebrities walked in. Ginny was excited and nervous. Hank picked up on this, as it was a departure from her usual high level of confidence.

"Hey, are you all right?" he asked her softly.

She smiled, nearly melting over the fact that he recognized that she was feeling slightly unsettled.

"Oh, Hank. So sweet of you to ask. It's just . . . Well, I haven't seen Mel since we all went our separate ways. And now I'm about to debut a song that he wrote and Nat recorded before anyone has even heard their version of it! I just hope it's a good idea, is all!"

Hank laughed. "Of course it's a good idea. It's *our* idea."

And with that, Ginny lit up like a Christmas tree.

She took the stage and wowed the audience with the worldwide debut of a song that would come to define Christmastime for generations. As she sang, she would occasionally steal a glance of Hank and he'd give her a wink. He'd shifted from winking at girls in the audience to winking at one who shared the bandstand with him. It was as though Ginny had everyone in the place under her spell and no one ever wanted the song to end.

Afterwards, Mel and Nat came backstage and could not stop talking about how beautiful it was, specifically complimenting the arrangement.

In his velvety tone, Nat kidded with his old pal Ginny, "Are you trying to show me up again?"

Ginny laughed and gave him a giant hug. "Fat chance of that."

Then she introduced them to Hank as the arranger, and they all said very flattering things to him. Hank was humbled because he knew the song was going to be a monster hit.

"You've written a real winner here. And Nat, I can't wait to hear you sing it," Hank said. Ginny was just so happy. Maybe happier than she'd ever been her whole life. It was the most wonderful way she could have ever dreamed of reuniting with Mel, and she knew she had Hank to thank for this emotional and wonderful evening. She felt like she was floating as they all slid into a booth and ordered several bottles of champagne.

The band had a few more shows in New York before Christmas. Tex kept "The Christmas Song" in the set for the season and it quickly became a crowd favorite. As soon as it hit the airwaves, audiences went crazy to hear it live. After a show one night, Hank went up to Ginny in the wings.

"It looks like your idea is working out really well," he said.

"Don't you mean *our* idea?" she smiled and winked.

"Touché. Would you like a glass of wine?" Hank asked.

"I'd love one."

They sat in the club after it had completely emptied out and had their first of many long talks.

"I can't tell you how good it felt the other night. Things just weren't left right, even though we all supported and understood Mel's decision to disband."

"Why did he want to break it all up?" Hank wondered.

"Oh, gosh, he's just so talented and there are so many things he wants to pursue. Acting, singing, radio, film, TV, writing . . . you name it."

"So, he has almost as much energy as you do!"

"More, if you can believe it!"

They laughed.

"But you know something? If it weren't for Mel's ambition, I wouldn't be sitting here right now with you. So, cheers to that," she said, raising her glass.

"Cheers to that."

They both took a healthy swig.

"When are you leaving to go back home to Los Angeles for Christmas?" Hank asked.

"Oh, I wish I could. I just can't afford the plane ticket."

"So, you'll be staying here in the city?"

"I suppose so."

"With no plans for Christmas?"

"Are you getting sentimental on me, Hank?"

"Well, that's just not right. You should come with me to Pennsylvania, where I'm going to visit my parents."

"Oh, I don't know."

"I insist. I'm not leaving you behind to be all alone on Christmas."

"You *insist*?"

"I do."

She leaned across the table and planted a giant kiss on his lips. He did not resist.

As they boarded a Pittsburgh-bound train at Grand Central Station, a woman was trying to manage several small children and a lot of luggage.

"*Déjà que te ayude*," Ginny said to the woman as she took one of the bags and the hand of one of the children. She found them a seat and placed the suitcase on the rack overhead.

"*Gracias. Eres muy amable*," the woman said.

"*De nada. Feliz Navidad*," Ginny said to the children.

Hank was dumbfounded. "You speak Spanish?"

"*Por supuesto*!"

Hank shook his head.

"I mean, *of course*. Spanish is my first language."

"I thought you were Irish. The name O'Connor was the tipoff there," Hank winked.

"That's Daddy's side. *Mi mama* is one hundred percent *Mexicana*."

"Well, no wonder you're such a fascination!"

Ginny smiled.

On the train ride, Ginny was happy to hear that Hank had come from humble beginnings just as she had. He'd told her about West Aliquippa and that his father had been a steel worker, just like the majority of the men in the town of immigrants.

"I never would have thought we had so much in common," she told Hank. "Both of our families struggled so much during the Depression. It's amazing that your parents were able to keep up your lessons through those years."

"My father was my first teacher, but it's always been his dream that I'd grow up to be a music teacher."

"Your father is a musician? My mother too."

"He's a flautist. Was professional for a time in Italy, so the legend goes. What does your mother play?"

"She's an amazing singer and pianist. She used to play in a department store demoing sheet music in exchange for my lessons."

"Wow. I suppose we're both blessed to have parents who held music in such high regard."

"Very blessed, indeed. I remember the very first song my mother taught me on piano. It's called 'Zacatecas,' the Mexican revolutionary song."

"I'd love to hear it sometime," Hank said.

"I always found a lot of peace and inspiration in that song."

"Well, if you love it, I'm sure I will too."

They arrived at the Mancini home in the afternoon and could smell Hank's mother's cooking from the curb outside. Quinto and Anna appeared on the front porch to greet them. One thing Ginny did not tell Hank was that she could never marry a man who didn't have a loving bond with his mother, so he was being tested without knowing it. Hank made the introductions and they all went inside. Right away, Ginny could see the sweetness and love between Hank and Anna. Quinto was a much harder nut to crack, just as advertised.

"Mr. Mancini, Hank tells me you are a wonderful flute and piccolo player. Would you play something for us?"

Ginny had read this just right. Without saying very much, Quinto went to the closet and pulled down one of the cases. He assembled the flautino and played an Italian folk song. Ginny was tickled and applauded when the song finished.

"I want to thank you for welcoming me into your home for Christmas," Ginny told them.

She went to the piano and played something for them. Then Hank took a seat next to her on the piano bench and they played Gershwin's duet, "I Got Rhythm." When it was over, they both laughed and sighed, feeling contented over one of the simple joys in life.

They returned to New York after Christmas for an engagement in New Jersey. The accommodations were in Manhattan, so they had to ride the subway back and forth to work. It was turning out to be a dreadful winter and, being from Southern California, little, brunette Ginny had only one coat. The commute gave them lots of time to sit and talk and continue to get to know each other.

"I'm sorry your parents split up," Hank said.

"To think that they met picking cherries. Something about that just breaks my heart. But my mother is happier, so . . ."

"What does your father do now?"

"He's a Teamster who drives trucks for Metro Goldwyn Mayer. It's a good union job, but the Depression was really tough on my family. I worked in an ice cream cone factory, a dry cleaner, and even a sheet metal company! But I lived for the Saturday matinees, where I could go if I saved up enough pennies. It was a great way to escape the harsh realities of life."

"When did you first get serious about singing?"

"Well, I always loved it, but I guess I realized I was pretty good at it by the time I got to high school and sang in the chorus. After I graduated from El Monte High, I went to Los Angeles City College and joined the chorus there. That's when I got really good at sight-reading. Mel said that's what really impressed him and it was the reason he hired me. I guess I'd just assumed it was a skill most singers had."

"Well, you certainly had a much more exciting upbringing than I did. With friends like Nat King Cole?!"

"Oh, and don't forget Sammy Davis Jr., Blake Edwards, and Judy Garland too."

"Okay, now you're just showing off."

"Maybe a little. Only to impress you, though."

"You can check that off your list."

She leaned over and kissed him. She couldn't help it—she was falling deeply in love. And all the talk about the movies reminded Hank about the time his father took him to see *The Crusades*.

"Oh, I love that film! Isn't it amazing?" Ginny remarked.

"I have a secret about it that I've never told anyone."

"Do tell!"

"Okay, but you have to promise not to laugh."

She crossed her heart.

"Well, first of all, my father called me a dummy—actually, a *cafone*—for thinking the music in the film was being played somewhere live in the movie theater," he began.

Ginny laughed just a little.

"No laughing!" he kidded her.

"But when the movie finished, I said to myself, 'I want to write music for the movies someday.'"

"Well, you must!" Ginny said, as though it were as easy as getting a job at Sears, Roebuck & Company.

"I appreciate your enthusiasm for my pipe dream."

She suddenly became dead serious. "It's no pipe dream, Henry. Film scoring is something that *someone* has to do. Why not someone as endlessly talented as you?"

Hank looked into her eyes and marveled at her ceaseless faith and belief in him.

"If you're really serious about this, you have to come to Hollywood. That's the place to pursue this and the time is now."

But Hank wasn't quite ready to leave the band.

The following spring, Ginny knew she couldn't face another

winter on the road and was ready to move back home. Knowing Hank would have many other suitors, she didn't feel she could ask him for a commitment.

"I can't do another winter out here," she told him.

"I understand," he said. "Can we write to each other?" he asked, knowing that neither of them could afford phone calls.

"I would love that."

They became very devoted pen pals and the time apart made them long for each other intensely. Then the day came that they decided they ought to get married. Hank went to Tex to give him the news.

"Congratulations, man! I think we all saw it comin' way before you did!"

"That's probably true!" Hank said. "I'll be moving out west at the end of the month."

"I can still use you as an arranger as long as you're available," Tex said.

"I'll need the work now more than ever!" Hank told him.

"Please send my congratulations to Ginny. I know you two will be very happy together."

"Thank you, Tex. For everything."

When Hank called Ginny that evening, she was a bit out of sorts.

"Tex sends his best wishes and is going to keep me as an arranger," he told her.

"That's wonderful," she said, but without her trademark cheeriness.

"What's the matter, my love?"

"Oh, I'm sorry. It's nothing. Just . . . my mother."

"What's wrong? Is she not well?" Hank asked.

"She doesn't approve."

"Well, I can't take it personally because we've never met. What is her objection, exactly?"

"She doesn't want me to marry a musician . . ." Ginny said.

"But she *is* a musician."

"She says she doesn't want me to starve."

Hank laughed, which made Ginny relax a little. "Then I'll just have to make sure you don't. In fact, I'm going to do my damnedest to make sure my wife doesn't ever want for a thing."

He could hear Ginny's sniffles on the other end of the line.

On his way out to California, Hank had a show in Cleveland, where he made plans to see his childhood friend Jack, who had also recently become engaged. Hank found out from his parents that Jack had moved there and was working as a band director at a high school. Hank called him up and invited Jack and his fiancée to his show, and they planned to meet beforehand to grab a bite. When Hank walked into the diner across the street from the venue, he found Jack and Dixie in a booth waiting for him. Hank beamed at the sight of his old pal, who threw his arms around him.

"You haven't changed a bit!" Jack said.

"Yup, same fedora and raincoat I had in high school! Depression baby!"

"Hank, I'd like you to meet my fiancée, Dixie."

"Very pleased to meet you, Dixie. I would like to compliment you on your excellent choice of a mate."

She laughed. "We ordered you a Coke," she said.

"Why, thank you. I actually have some news as well . . ."

"Oh, really?" Jack was curious.

"I'm engaged too!"

Dixie raised her Coca-Cola to toast.

"Congratulations! Who is the lucky lady?" Jack asked.

"Her name is Ginny O'Connor, from Los Angeles. She was a singer in the Mello-Larks—that's how we met."

"Oh, the Mello-Larks are fabulous!" Dixie said. "But she's not singing with them anymore?"

"It was time for her to get off the road. It's much too cold out here for a Southern California girl."

"So, you'll be moving to Los Angeles, then?"

"I'm on my way there now."

"Oh, that's exciting, Hank. Good for you. Dixie and I wish you and Ginny every happiness."

"Thanks, Jack. And we wish you both the same."

"What will you do out there?"

"Ginny seems to think I might be able to get work in the movie business."

"How thrilling!" Dixie said.

"If nothing else, I can work on my tan."

Chapter Six

A LIFE IN TUNE

When Hank arrived in Los Angeles, he moved in with Ginny and her mother, who lived in Rosemead, a few miles east of downtown. There he slept on the sofa until he and Ginny were married and could find a place of their own. Ginny's mother, despite not officially approving of their marriage, was happy that her daughter was marrying a fellow who was Catholic and would be married in a Catholic church—the family parish where Ginny went to school and made her first communion, the Church of the Blessed Sacrament in Hollywood. It was a joyful ceremony on September 13, 1947. Ginny told Hank that she had always dreamed of being married there. Ginny's mother struggled to save about $3,000 to pay for the reception of 250 guests at the old Brunswick Mansion on posh West Adams Boulevard south of downtown. Champagne was not in the budget, so they got creative and served white wine topped with ginger ale. Great music made up for any of the wedding's shortcomings.

The couple honeymooned in Las Vegas for a week and returned to Los Angeles to move into an apartment on Parrish Place in Burbank for $90 a month. As Depression babies, Hank and Ginny got along remarkably well with very little money. They were both naturally contented people who appreciated the little things, such as the intoxicating scent of orange blossoms in the San Fernando Valley that Hank thought seemed to be everywhere. It was a far cry from the smell of the steel plant he grew up next to in West Aliquippa. Yes, he thought, this California lifestyle would suit him just fine. The only trick was going to be finding enough work to properly support himself and his new bride.

The first roadblock to this was finding out that the American Federation of Musicians Local 47 required him to wait six months for his union card. While he waited, he put his GI bill to use and began studying at the Westlake School of Music in Hollywood. Opened in 1945, Westlake was the first academic institution—after the Schillinger House in Boston, which later became the Berklee School of Music—to offer a degree based on the study of jazz. It became a prototype of jazz education for other colleges looking to make a name for themselves in this area, such as Los Angeles City College, where Ginny attended, and North Texas State University. While studying, Hank also continued to do some arranging for Tex at $50 per score, which helped add to the $52 per week in unemployment he received.

The biggest upside to living in Los Angeles was Ginny's vast network of friends and contacts. She wasted no time introducing Hank to everyone and made no secret of his talents and ambitions. One of the first people she connected Hank with was Harry Zimmerman, a composer, conductor, and arranger for radio shows on the Mutual Radio Network. *The Family Theater* was a show of dramatizations of classic books, sponsored by the Archdiocese of Los Angeles. Harry found Hank delightful and was in great need of help with all the shows he had going, so he hired him to score *A Tale of Two Cities*—Hank's first drama assignment. Hank had absolutely no idea what he was doing, but as with everything else, he applied his strong work ethic and learned on the job. Ginny jumped back into doing studio sessions as a singer and worked consistently, but money was still tight, which meant there was no way for them to go out with friends. They couldn't afford living room furniture and spent most of their time waiting for the phone to ring—the neighbor's phone, that is.

Another of Ginny's friends soon became an important person in Hank's professional life. A wonderful choreographer named Nick Castle had begun working with talent who was gushing out of Hollywood's star system in its last days. Suddenly, many actors who once had contracts with studios were no longer earning a steady salary. But for the people who could sing and dance, like Betty Hutton, who played Annie Oakley in *Annie Get Your Gun*, there was plenty of work with all the new nightclubs springing up in Lake Tahoe, Reno, and Las Vegas. Nick Castle quickly became a huge fan of Hank's writing and began hiring him to do some arranging for these nightclub acts. Nick soon began to see Hank as a good friend and felt a duty to help explain the lay of the land as Hank was brand new to the business of Hollywood. As they sat working at a coffee shop near Nick's studio one day, Nick told Hank something very important.

"Your arranging skills are first rate, Hank. And you work incredibly fast," Nick complimented him. "But there's something you need to think about—arrangers only get paid once. Composers get paid each and every time that their work is used for profit. Selfishly, I don't want to lose you as an arranger. But this is something you need to consider moving forward."

"Gee, Nick. I don't know why I never thought of that. How exactly do the composers get paid each time?"

"Through an outfit called ASCAP—American Society of Composers, Authors and Publishers. They monitor all the usage in radio, film, stage, and television and collect for their members."

"I'll look into it right away. Coffee's on me," Hank said with a smile.

Hank went home and wasted no time writing a letter to ASCAP to find out how to become a member. He received a reply a couple weeks later that explained that he would need to have one of his original works played on radio or television, or have a song published. He knew that there was no possible way at that time that he could have sped up getting a song on television or radio as much as he would have liked to, but he also realized there was nothing preventing him from setting up his own publishing company to publish and print the music himself. This kind of proactive business acumen was just the beginning of all the other groundbreaking moves that would follow as his career unfolded. When Ginny returned home after a session, she found Hank typing up letterhead for his new publishing company while putting the finishing touches on his first song to be published through this entity.

"It's a terribly dumb song," Hank told her.

She laughed. "I'll be the judge of that. What's this dumb song of yours called?"

"'The Soft-Shoe Boogie.'"

"Now, that's just adorable," she said, putting her arms

around him. She picked up the sheet music and, with her expert sight-reading skills, began humming the melody as she danced a little soft-shoe.

"Not half as adorable as you are," Hank smiled slyly.

He had five hundred copies of his little ditty printed, piled them up in his closet, and voilà! He was the newest member of ASCAP.

Of the many artists Nick introduced Hank to, the most well known was Buddy Rich, a talented singer and dancer as well as an excellent drummer. Buddy had been performing in a vaudeville act since he was a child and would go through periods of not playing drums to go back to song and dance. Hank wrote an entire show for Buddy—thirty minutes of music, which included a lot of orchestration, pages and pages of notes, and untold hours at the piano. Having grown up in a family of professional performers made it all the more shocking when Buddy wouldn't pay Hank. He and Ginny needed the money desperately, so Hank felt he had no choice but to report Buddy to the union. Buddy eventually paid, and he and Hank even became friends. Only once, years later, did he ever reference the incident, along with his apology: "Sorry you had to wait, babe."

As Hank and Ginny's one-year wedding anniversary approached, Ginny got some exciting news from her old pals in the Mello-Larks, who wanted to know if she would join them for a monthlong engagement at the London Palladium. The idea was very appealing to her, having never traveled abroad before. But a moment later, she panicked when she realized what the dates away would mean.

"Hank, I don't know! I want to do it, but I would be away for our first anniversary. I know what a great opportunity it is and all, and that we could use the money too. But . . ."

"But what?" he asked.

"Well, it breaks my heart a little to think of us not being together on our very first anniversary. That only happens once."

"The second anniversary also only happens once. And, come to think of it, the same goes for the third, the fourth, and the fifth. They'll all be special and they'll all only happen once."

She laughed. "I suppose that's true."

"Sweetheart, you might always regret it if you don't go," Hank said. "And I plan on celebrating many, many more anniversaries with you."

"You won't be disappointed?"

"We'll celebrate before you go and after you get back."

"I'll still be a sad mess on the actual day," she confessed.

"I'm not saying I won't miss you terribly," he smiled, putting his arms around her.

The truth was, Hank missed Ginny the minute she left. On September 13, 1948, Ginny found two dozen roses in her cold, crummy London dressing room and, just as she predicted, began to weep. She pulled herself together just before showtime and thought of how soon it would be before she'd be back in the California sunshine with her beloved Hank. It was difficult to even talk on the phone very much because of their schedules and the time difference. Back home, Hank had been hired to do some shows at another Palladium—this one in Hollywood—with the Art Mooney Orchestra. Part of the act was the band singing Mooney's big hit "I'm Looking Over a Four Leaf Clover" while Hank played glockenspiel. Maybe it was because singing was the one thing Hank didn't really do and therefore did not enjoy, but he grew to detest the job and began throwing in some wrong notes during that tune, which got him fired.

Hank made up for it by picking up all the other work that

came his way and soon there was more good news from the Mello-Larks.

"The Mello-Larks have been asked to appear in a short subject film they're doing at Universal!" Ginny shouted excitedly.

When the group went to the studio for their first meeting with Joe Gershenson, head of Universal's music department, Ginny learned some important information.

"You can start rehearsals with the director as soon as we can get some arrangements done for the songs," Gershenson said.

"When do you think that will be?" Ginny asked.

"As soon as we assign an arranger."

"We have our very own arranger, who is quite good," she smiled.

"Who is that?" Joe asked.

"Henry Mancini. Maybe you've heard of him?" she asked.

Ginny introduced Hank to Joe Gershenson and, just like that, Hank landed his first movie job, working on the same project with his very talented wife. Part of him couldn't actually believe he was going to be working *in the movie business*—a dream he'd nurtured since he was a young boy in that opulent movie house back in Pennsylvania watching *The Crusades*. The other part of him was already such a consummate professional that working in the movie business suddenly felt somewhat normal once it had become a reality. He was prepared for this and he knew there was only one chance to make a first impression. So, in tackling the assignment for a "hip, clean, and cool" arrangement of "Skip to My Lou," Hank instinctively knew exactly what to do. He played it for Ginny and she thought it was terrific. The boss loved it too. Ginny was incredibly proud of her husband and it only reinforced what she had long known—that his talent would be recognized and rewarded.

~

Quinto and Anna called to tell Hank that they were planning a drive across the country to visit. Hank knew this would mean his parents would be staying in the apartment with them, despite not having enough room for guests. As soon as his parents arrived, they fell in love with Southern California.

"It is so much like Italy," Anna said. "Everyone is growing their own oranges and lemons and herbs. It is so lovely."

"Hank has been doing such great work and meeting so many influential people," Ginny told them as she served a dinner of homemade enchiladas.

"What about your degree?" Quinto asked pointedly.

It seemed there was nothing that would convince his father he was on a good path.

"I've earned some additional credits through the classes I took at the Westlake School of Music. But I also need to focus on work and taking the jobs that come my way," Hank told him.

Quinto grunted. "You need to finish your degree. That is something real."

Hank and Ginny exchanged a look.

"Also, we think it will be better for your mother's health for us to come here."

Hank and Ginny were very surprised. Anna looked very happy to hear her husband say this, even though Hank could tell it was the first time she was hearing about it.

"You mean move? Here?" Hank asked. "Of course!"

Ginny smiled. "It would be lovely to be surrounded by more of our family," she added.

Quinto and Anna went home and packed up their belongings

to return to the paradise of California. Over dinner with Ginny one night, Hank was suddenly struck by a thought.

"Oh, no."

"What is it, dear?" Ginny asked.

"Do you think my father thinks they are going to live with us?"

"Why would he think that?"

"That's how they do things in the old country."

"But we don't have the room. Especially now that . . ." She smiled the widest smile Hank had ever seen on her face.

"Now that?"

"Now that we're expecting."

"Oh, Gin!"

Ginny would never forget Hank's expression at that moment. He was so happy, she thought he might cry. On July 2, 1950, their son Christopher was born.

Hank continued to pick up work wherever he could and soon came to learn just how much he'd impressed Joe Gershenson. Like all studio executives, Joe had an assistant who knew almost more than the boss did. This man was Milt Rosen, who had great instincts and was very familiar with Hank's background writing for swing bands. Milt knew Hank's sensibilities would bring something fresh to the studio's upcoming movie musical projects—certainly more so than any composer of strictly European symphonic scoring could. Milt discussed this with Joe, who had been looking for someone with just this mix of a dance-band mindset but who also knew a little something about strings. Joe summoned Hank to an editing suite.

"I've got a test assignment for you, if you're interested," Joe told Hank.

"Sure! What is it?"

"This is the new Abbott and Costello called *Lost in Alaska*."

"Love those guys," Hank said without getting too excited about scoring a scene with the comedy legends.

"Roll the film?" Joe instructed the editor.

"Here's the scene we need scored."

Hank watched the flickering black and white images of Lou Costello getting bit on his backside by a crab.

"What do you think? You wanna take a crack at this crab?"

"You bet!" Hank replied.

"I can pay you $225 a week and we'll need it in two weeks."

"And you'll have it!"

Hank approached working on this ridiculous scene as seriously as if he were scoring *War and Peace*. It paid off—Joe was thrilled with the work. Hank felt that if he was patient and just kept hitting assignments out of the park, other good things would follow. He used what little money he had to help buy his parents a house when they arrived in California. He purchased them a tiny place in the city of Bell on the way to Long Beach. Even that didn't seem to improve his relationship with his father, who still didn't understand why Hank wasn't back in college earning that music degree.

"What will you do when you can't find any more work in music?" Quinto asked him. "Teaching is something that will always be there."

There was nothing he could really say to make his father understand. It was difficult to explain the way building a career in Hollywood worked to anyone outside of it. The move to California failed to improve Anna's health as hoped, and she suffered a series of eight heart attacks. It devastated Hank to watch her rapid decline. He and Ginny made the two-hour drive to see them once a week and Anna was very grateful that she lived long enough to see her first grandchild being born. Hank's father only grew angrier, unable to cope with his wife's frail state of health. Hank rushed to his mother's side when it looked as though she would not be able to bounce back. He held her tiny hands in his.

"Mamma, I love you so much. I hope you know that," he whispered.

"I love you, *mio angelo prezioso*," she mustered faintly.

He reached up to stroke her face and she slipped away, her slight smile lingering for a moment. Hank felt as if he were frozen in time as tears began to stream down his face. Either he couldn't or wouldn't move from her side, as the shock of her being gone took him over. He'd never felt this way before—like a rock had replaced his heart in his chest. In the days and months that followed, he was plunged into a deep sadness that he had never before experienced. Because he was earning a bit more money, he and Ginny decided to move his father into a nice mobile home so he could be closer to them. A short time later, Ginny got pregnant again—this time with twins. Hank was overjoyed and he also knew he was going to have to figure out a way to keep earning.

Chapter Seven

FULL CIRCLE MOMENT

Based on the stellar work Hank had done scoring the infamous crab scene, he was offered a staff composer position at Universal. He and Ginny were relieved he would be earning a steady income, but completely overjoyed for him to be pursuing what was no longer a secret dream. It seemed that Hank's hard work was really beginning to pay off. The bigger win, of course, was the timing—Hank was getting into the film scoring business at exactly the right time and the right place, just as Ginny once foretold back on one of those train rides while they were touring with the Glenn Miller Orchestra.

The timing was critical due to the fact that the position Hank was hired for, a staff composer, no longer exists at any major Hollywood film studio and hasn't for a very long time. In those days, Universal was making about fifty pictures a year. It was king of the B movie, a category that came to be associated with low-budget creature features, science fiction, and other genre films with titles such as *Monster on the Campus*, *The Thing*

That Couldn't Die, and *Tarantula*. These were movies made fast and cheap through an assembly line process. Despite the fact that B movies were oftentimes equated with low production values, this is not where the name came from. Rather, it was during the heyday of the double feature, and the B movie was the one billed with the main feature and designed to have a shorter running time of usually around an hour. In the music department, a film would be divvied up amongst many staff composers, who were tasked with creating themes or writing separate music cues for the movie. Then, once all the various parts were completed, it could be assembled into the final product.

While these films were not winning any awards, the system afforded Hank the opportunity of a lifetime to learn the craft with a hands-on paid position. He mastered every trick of the trade and was able to adapt quickly, working on everything from the *Francis the Talking Mule* and *Bonzo the Chimp* franchises to far more prestigious pictures—about 120 films in his six years there, or roughly twenty films a year. The fact that he was not able to choose his own projects forced him to get a firm grasp on writing for every style and genre—drama, comedy, suspense, horror, and everything in between. While this kind of workload would be impossible for one person, as part of a team, it provided these staff composers with vast exposure and experience. Part of the job was also writing source music whenever it was required, which is any music that comes from a source within the film, such as a jukebox, radio, or band. Every day brought a new musical challenge and Hank relished it. One of his greatest musical mentors at the studio was Universal's only staff orchestrator, David Tamkin.

"Every time I'm called into Tamkin's office, it's like making up for the orchestration classes I'd been unable to take at Juilliard," Hank told Ginny one night after work.

"You love your job, don't you?" she asked.

"Can you tell?" Hank winked.

The whole process would begin with Joe Gershenson calling in a couple of the staff guys to *spot* the picture, which meant determining where each piece of music would go. Once in a while, the producer of the film would take part in these spotting sessions, but most of the time they were already off making their next picture somewhere else on the lot, so this was entirely left up to the music department. For the ultra-low-budget movies, an entirely different process took place. *Cribbing* involved pillaging the Universal music library for scores that the studio already owned to find music cues that could be repurposed for another film. Whenever Hank was called upon to do this, he learned another extremely important aspect of film scoring, which, in film parlance, is referred to as having music *play against* picture. This is when the image contrasts heavily with the music in order to create unexpected results. Hank was very taken with the discovery of the idea that sometimes the most downright chilling effects are achieved this way. The example he often referenced was from the film *The Victors*, in which Frank Sinatra's recording of "Have Yourself a Merry Little Christmas" is used in a scene depicting the execution of a GI deserter in a snowy Belgian field. Hank would famously play against picture later in his career to great effect. Cribbing also forced him to listen to and learn from these older and often terrific scores. Ironically, the best music in the Universal library was frequently used to score the cheapest movies in order to counterbalance their low production values.

On the home front, carrying the twins was proving to be a

difficult pregnancy for Ginny. It was an enormous relief when their delivery went so smoothly. On May 4, 1952, Hank and Ginny welcomed the girls, with Monica born first and Felice arriving five minutes later. The newborns were brought home to join two-year-old Chris, who was getting into everything as toddlers do, and Hank and Ginny began to rethink the size of their family.

"You know how we always thought we'd have four children?" Ginny asked Hank one morning when all three children were crying.

"Did we say that?" he asked.

"We did, but I'm not sure what we were thinking! It sounds like a tragic opera in the other room," she said, laughing and on the verge of tears.

Hank wrapped her in his arms. "I am perfectly happy with our little trio."

"Good. Because it might be all I can handle."

Raising the children became more than a full-time job for Ginny. She decided that she needed to give up her singing career, at least for the time being. Hank helped her at home as much as he could as she struggled to keep up with all the feedings, cloth diapers, and the extraordinary demands of twins. While at work, Hank was proving himself a worthy hire and Ginny was a great source of inspiration for him. She was a wellspring of joy and positivity. Having both grown up with modest means made it so that when they could afford to buy their own home, it was all the more meaningful. After moving out of their first apartment on Parrish Place, they lived for a short time in Toluca Lake, an idyllic neighborhood in Burbank, and then found a home to buy in North Hollywood, still close to the studio. The house was a two-bedroom with a den, where the babies would share a room and Hank would have a place to work. It never ceased to amaze Ginny how well Hank could maintain his focus when working at home in the midst of the pandemonium. It was precisely this work ethic that prepared him for his first major break.

In 1954, two years into his time at Universal, Hank was given an assignment on what would wind up being one of the most iconic science fiction films of all time, *Creature from the Black Lagoon*. Even though Hank shared the work with four other composers, it is notable that he was given the lion's share of the responsibility on this film. It also marks the time when he began to create some of his most breathtakingly romantic and ethereal pieces that would go on to inspire other composers and filmmakers for many years to come. As if there had been any doubt left in Joe Gershenson's mind about the depth of Hank's talent, he'd vanquished it with his work on *Creature from the Black Lagoon*. After completing his assigned cues for the film, Joe called Hank to his office.

"Hank! Come on in. Have a seat! Say, I've been meaning to ask you . . . didn't you work with Glenn Miller during the war?"

"Sadly, I never got the chance. I met with him just after I'd joined up hoping to get into the band he was putting together for the Army Air Corps. It was terrifying going to see him—he was at the peak of his career. Today, that would be like a nineteen-year-old kid going to meet Elvis. He didn't pick me, but he probably saved my life."

"How so?"

"He recommended me for a different Air Corps band, which kept me out of gunnery school. Without Glenn Miller, I might have been fire-hosed out of a ball turret or the tail of a B-17."

Gershenson paused for a moment to let that sink in. "Then I can't think of anyone better to write the score for the story of his life," he smiled.

"No kidding?" Hank said in disbelief, hoping that this meant what he thought it meant—that he would be writing the entire score himself, even though he would be sharing screen credit with Joe, as the head of the music department.

"Well, I can't think of anyone better. Can you?"

"Come to think of it, no!"

They chuckled and then Hank got very serious for a moment. "Thank you, Joe. This is an incredible opportunity and a real honor."

It was a full-circle moment when the old cliché *everything happens for a reason* seemed to ring loud and true. Hank left Gershenson's office on top of the world and rushed home. He walked into the house to find Ginny juggling the babies. He kissed her, took Chris off her hands, and tossed him into the air.

"You're not going to believe this," he said in a low tone of excitement.

"What is it, darling?"

"Joe Gershenson offered me my own film."

"Oh, that's wonderful, Hank!"

He marveled at the way she spun around from child to child, tending to them as though it were all part of some elaborately choreographed dance, making his work look easy.

"After just two years? My, you are impressive," Ginny said.

"Glad you think so."

They laughed.

"What film?"

"That part's the real kicker!"

"Wait a minute," she said, searching her memory and then taking a wild guess. "Is it *The Glenn Miller Story*?"

"How did you know?!" Sometimes Hank was downright spooked by Ginny's omniscience.

"I read *The Hollywood Reporter* most days while the babies are napping."

"I wonder who will be playing him in the film. It sure would be great if he is an actual musician as well as actor."

"My sources tell me it's going to be Jimmy Stewart."

Hank was astounded. He couldn't think of anyone better despite Stewart not being a musician. Movie magic would fix that!

"Shall I open some wine to toast the occasion?"

"You betcha," Ginny said with a wink.

As production on *The Glenn Miller Story* began, Hank was impressed that Jimmy Stewart hired a trombone coach named Joe Yukl to teach him to play Dixieland trombone. Jimmy's goal was to be able to actually play in the scenes portraying Miller with his orchestra. The production was given Glenn Miller's actual trombone on loan from the National Museum of the US Air Force, but even that was not enough to inspire any latent musical ability Stewart may have had. Before long, his teacher was practically living with him and going a bit crazy from listening to Stewart's novice efforts around the clock as the actor tried valiantly to get a handle on such a difficult instrument. Joe ended up doing the actual playing while Jimmy pretended for the camera. His brilliant miming more than made up for his musical shortcomings, as he absolutely mastered the handling of the instrument down to the minutest details—including the gesture associated with blowing the spit out of the valve. As one of the few people on the production team who had actually met the real Glenn Miller, Hank was incredibly impressed at how well Jimmy channeled his subject, right down to Miller's tense smile.

Hank began working on the score at home on his rented upright piano. Some days, he got to thinking deeply about Miller's life and couldn't help but be moved at what a mark he'd left on the world, despite not being in it nearly long enough. In these moments, he would pace, pipe in hand, and talk it through with Ginny.

"It's incredibly tragic he had to go so young," Hank said. "Think about all the music he had left to create."

"It's terribly sad. What do you think happened to his plane?"

"Most thought friendly fire at first. But in the years since, I've heard from some service buddies that it was more likely a faulty carburetor—the plane he was on had the kind that was known to freeze up in cold weather."

"As he was on his way to perform for our troops stationed in France?"

Hank reflected on that heartbreaking thought for a moment. "I've been thinking that maybe the film should have an original song. A love theme, you know, for Glenn and Helen. Glenn's hits will be used in the film's montages but they don't exactly fit for their love story. Is that incredibly presumptuous on my part?"

"No. Why would you think that?" Ginny asked.

"Oh, I don't know. A song that he didn't write and that the audience won't know?"

"It's the movies, Hank. Anything goes that serves the story. Pitch the idea to Joe. I'm pretty sure he'll love it."

"It'll be a love theme featuring trombone, of course. What do you think of the title 'Too Little Time'?"

"I love it."

Joe Gershenson was somewhat neutral about the idea of an original song, saying, "Sure, Hank. Go write one."

Instinctively, Hank was creating an opportunity for himself. Writing "Too Little Time" would show what a formidable melodist he was, a skill that was not all that common in composers, whose minds have to consider music in a larger global sense. Gifted melodists are a prized rarity. As soon as Hank finished writing the song, he played it first for Ginny, who was moved to tears.

"This is such an inspired idea, Hank. I can't imagine the film *without* this song."

"Remember to imagine trombone playing the melody," he said.

"That's a little harder, but I trust you!"

The song was sweeping, epic, and romantic. Somehow it seemed to effortlessly and poignantly capture the preciousness of time without veering into melodrama. In time, this quintessential Mancini touch would be heard again and again—pure elegance without over sentimentalizing. The morning after the premiere of the film that February, Ginny read the newspaper to Hank.

"It says here that Glenn Miller's mother attended the premiere," she told him as she read the article.

Hank poured himself a cup of coffee and picked up another section of the paper.

"It's a cruel trick of nature whenever parents outlive their children. I sure hope she was pleased with the film," he said.

"Well, let's see. It says here, 'while she enjoyed the movie, she thought that her son was better looking than Jimmy Stewart.'"

They laughed heartily.

Up to that point, film biographies about musicians had not done well at the box office. But *The Glenn Miller Story*, with its tagline, "The story of a love that made wonderful music," was both a critical and commercial success—so much so that it led to the studio green-lighting *The Benny Goodman Story* starring Steve Allen. Joe Gershenson assigned Hank to work on this one as well. Unlike Glenn Miller, at the time the film about his life was being made, Benny Goodman was still alive and his band was reunited to rerecord everything for the film. When Hank first crossed paths with Goodman on the Universal lot, the King of Swing failed to remember him from the fiasco at the Paramount in New York, or when Max Adkins first introduced them in his dressing room at the Stanley Theatre in Pittsburgh. For this, Hank was grateful. It was like they were meeting for the first time.

The year 1954 was shaping up to be an exceptional one for Hank. With the money he was making, he put Quinto on the payroll as a music librarian and bought him a new car. Yet Quinto could never seem to understand why he wasn't living with Hank and Ginny and their family. And if he was at all impressed with any of the things Hank was doing, he certainly did not let on about it.

"Hey, Pop, I'm going to be working with one of Ginny's childhood friends next week, the great Sammy Davis Jr.! What do you think of that?"

"Have you thought about when you are going to go back to school?"

"Not really, Pop. I'm just too busy right now. And that's a good thing!"

Sammy Davis Jr. was asked to sing on a song for Universal's upcoming film *Six Bridges to Cross* starring Tony Curtis. Sammy was a recording artist with Decca Records, which by that time had taken full control of Universal, so it was a cross promotion that made sense. At the time, Sammy was in the midst of a monthlong engagement in Las Vegas singing with the Will Mastin Trio, comprised of Will Mastin, Sammy Davis Sr., and Sammy Davis Jr.—the latter had taken the place of Howard Colbert Jr., who'd been Sammy Jr.'s tap dance teacher and was like an uncle to him. For the *Six Bridges to Cross* session, Sammy planned to drive in from Vegas for the day to record at Universal.

"I'm so excited for you to meet and work with Sammy. He's the sweetest," Ginny told Hank. "The last time we spoke, he told me he was in a really good place with everything in Vegas."

"I can imagine that hasn't always been easy for him."

"Do you know the New Frontier Hotel and Casino used to expect him and his father to stay in the most rundown part of town, miles from the Strip?"

"During the run of their engagement?" Hank asked quizzically.

"Yes!"

"There's no excuse for that kind of behavior."

"I know it. But now, Sammy says, they are staying in the best rooms at the New Frontier. And he says that even the Las Vegas police have begun to treat him hospitably."

"That's progress, then," Hank said.

"He's absolutely over the moon about recording his first movie soundtrack."

"It's going to be great," Hank said excitedly.

On the day of the session, Sammy did not arrive on time. Hank did his best to stall and work on setting up and tweaking the arrangement, but he began to grow concerned. He didn't know if he should reschedule the session in order to stop the clock running on all the studio musicians, or if there was a chance that Sammy might walk in the door any moment. He called Ginny.

"Gin, I'm at the studio and Sammy hasn't shown up," Hank said. "He was supposed to be here hours ago."

"What? Sammy is never late to anything. Never."

That's when Hank got a sinking feeling that something was very wrong. He hung up with Ginny and went to speak to the studio executives to enlist their assistance.

He took the elevator up to the top floor of the famous black tower on the Universal lot and into the executive suites of the studio brass. One of the production executives saw him in the hallway and called him into his office.

"Hank, what can I do for you?" he said.

"Well, we've got everyone sitting around, waiting to start this session with Sammy Davis Jr., who's now," he looked down at his watch, "a little over three hours late. My wife has known Sammy for years and she says there's just no chance he would ever be late, unless something happened that was out of his control."

"You're right, Hank. Sammy's known for being a staunch professional."

"He was driving in from Las Vegas just for the session, so maybe he had some car trouble and might be stranded out in the middle of the desert, for all we know."

The man behind the desk got an idea. "I think I might still have a contact in the Nevada Sherriff's Department. Let me make a call."

"Great. Thank you," Hank said and waited.

Sure enough, something had gone terribly wrong.

"I see," Hank heard the executive say on the phone. "Thank you very much. We'll contact the hospital right away."

He hung up and turned to Hank.

"Sammy's been in accident. I'm very sorry, Hank. He's in a hospital in San Bernardino. It seems he may have lost an eye."

Ginny was devastated to hear the news about her childhood friend and extended her support to Sammy and his family. After the accident, Sammy became despondent, believing that his career was going to grind to a halt just after he'd begun to make big strides. That feeling didn't last long, though. After a pep talk from his pal Frank Sinatra, he bounced back. Frank told Sammy he had two choices—either let the loss of his eye keep him down forever, or fight back and achieve greatness. Sammy chose the latter, and during his first public appearance after the accident, Sinatra, Dean Martin, and others appeared onstage with him—all wearing eye patches.

Nearly a year after *The Glenn Miller Story* was released, Hank received a call in the predawn hours one day late in January. The music from *The Glenn Miller Story* had been nominated for an Academy Award. A sleepy Ginny rolled over when she realized what it was about—neither of them had been expecting this and hadn't exactly been thinking about the fact that the nominations were coming out. She squealed with excitement, kissing and congratulating Hank. He hung up the phone and turned to her.

"I can't believe it," he said, nearly shell-shocked.

"I can!"

"I would have never seen this day without you, Gin."

"Nonsense. All I had to do was convince you to move here."

Everyone from the craftspeople to those in the black tower at Universal were incredibly proud of Hank. Ginny now had the welcome problem of having nothing to wear to the Oscars. In those days, the Academy Awards ceremony was held at the Pantages Theatre on Hollywood Boulevard. A historic art deco theater, it was the last to be built by the vaudeville impresario Alexander Pantages, and opened in 1930. It had been one of Ginny's favorite childhood haunts. During those Depression years, it operated primarily as a movie theater, with live entertainment presented only occasionally. Ginny found a stunning gown at a small shop in Burbank and Hank rented a tuxedo for the evening.

Walking down the red carpet was utterly surreal for both of them—Ginny felt like a young girl living in a dream and Hank was also transported back in time to the Stanley Theatre in Pittsburgh, where he was first inspired to write movie music. Now here he was, nominated for an Academy Award. There was a whole host of emotions and thoughts running through his mind—gratitude toward his parents, Max Adkins, Tex Beneke, and Joe and Milt from Universal; sadness that his mother was no longer alive to see this day; and humility at a time when many other people in his shoes were feeling pride. He had absolutely no expectations of winning—simply being nominated was beyond anything he could have ever imagined. Everyone seated near him and Ginny congratulated him on the nomination. As exuberant as Ginny was, Hank could also tell she was not happy about being seated next to the actor Milton Berle, who was smoking a cigar all night.

~

Hank didn't let the honor of receiving an Oscar nomination create any kind of overblown idea about himself. Instead, he took on the next unique challenge the studio threw at him, which was writing for Universal's first rock musical, *Rock, Pretty Baby*. It was a movie about a young man who sells his law books in order to buy an electric guitar and pursue his dreams of becoming a rock star. Hank had a lot of fun writing songs for this film. It was such a departure from everything else he had worked on up to that point. After hearing Hank's music for the film, Liberty Records felt he would be the perfect candidate to showcase their new technology, the Spectra-Sonic Sound recording process, which claimed to be the ultimate in high-fidelity sound recording at the time. They offered him a recording contract to make an album that he called *Driftwood and Dreams*, which included an eerie but groovy version of "Bali Ha'i" from the musical *South Pacific*. That song set the tone for the rest of the record, which employed evocative, haunting background vocals to achieve a downright moony, astral effect that transports the listener to a deserted tropical island. With this recording, Hank was able to release a pop album under his own name, achieving another major career milestone. Feeling that he'd earned significant creative capital with this undertaking, Hank began to lobby the studio for more single-credit dramatic scores.

Unaware that he was nearing the end of his time at Universal, Hank landed a coveted assignment in 1957 when he was put on *Touch of Evil* for director Orson Welles. This project was a tremendous shift for the studio that had been associated with much less serious fare. Hank was thrilled to have the opportunity to work with a director as revered as Orson Welles. His 1941 masterpiece *Citizen Kane* solidified his place in film history as one of the greatest directors, after receiving unanimous critical praise. There was no one in the entire industry who wouldn't have jumped at the chance to work with such a legend.

During production of *Touch of Evil*, Welles wrote a three-page letter to Joe Gershenson that detailed what he wanted for the music. Hank had been studying the script closely and was beginning to see rushes of the film—the raw footage that was shot each day. It turned out that he was developing exactly the same concept for the music as Welles, who wasn't interested in traditional underscore, or the disembodied music that is not part of the world of the film, per se. He wanted to bring out the realism of the setting of Mexico and have all the music play as source that was coming from the bars, clubs, and radios of the streets where most of the scenes take place. The director described a roving camera that would pick up a series of different Latin jazz tunes emanating from a succession of the loudspeakers that the clubs that pumped music through to attract customers. All of Hank's experience writing source music for other Universal films culminated in this extraordinary film.

Touch of Evil created another wonderful chance for Hank to show his talent and enormous creativity. The first thing he realized about his approach to this film was that the Universal orchestra was not going to cut it, as wonderfully skilled as they were. He knew this project was going to demand a new caliber of players who were the best of the best, and Hank broke completely new ground by bringing in jazz musicians. The brass instruments in particular would be critical for creating the dark mood of the film. Hank went to Joe to tell him his plan for going outside the normal channels to line up an impressive list of pedigreed jazz players for what would become the first true Mancini jazz score.

"We're going to have to hire an actual big band," Hank said. "This stuff is going to need to sound like a Latin big band, like Stan Kenton's."

"That's an interesting approach, Hank. Who d'you have in mind?"

"Shelly Manne on drums, for sure, whom you know and have worked with . . ."

"Love Shelly," Joe said.

"And I'd like to get Jack 'Mr. Bongo' Costanzo on bongos. And we're going to need a big brass section. Conrad Gozzo on trumpet, maybe."

Hank also enlisted Plas Johnson on saxophone, who would later go on to make a tremendous splash when he played the lead sax part on *The Pink Panther* theme. Hank got Red Norvo on vibes, and additional West Coast jazz sax players Dave Pell and Barney Kessel on guitar. The band Hank assembled for *Touch of Evil* was magnificent.

Tremendous tension had been developing between the studio and Welles during production of the film. Hank went to observe some of the shooting in Venice Beach, and was so unobtrusive that Orson didn't even know he was there. In fact, Hank didn't realize then that Orson didn't even know who he was. Toward the end of the shoot, Hank felt there should be a meeting to discuss the music with the director and it was arranged. One rainy Saturday, Orson blew into Joe Gershenson's office on a cloud of his own Montecristo cigar smoke, cloaked in a black cape and hat. Throughout the making of the film, Orson had been especially at loggerheads with the producer, Al Zugsmith. Al was a fast-talking, slick Hollywood archetype, completely incompatible with Orson's erudite, artistic temperament. At one point during the meeting, Al made a comment at which Orson visibly bristled. Everyone in the room could see him try to let it go, but he just couldn't. Hank watched Orson closely as he got more and more agitated with each passing moment, until he finally blew his stack and lashed out, yelling "Who is *that* guy?" and pointing to Hank. It did not seem to matter that they'd been introduced at the beginning of the meeting just thirty minutes earlier.

The score for *Touch of Evil* would forever remain one of Hank's best by his own estimation, even though Orson Welles eventually walked off the project when the studio took over the cut of his film. Hank didn't think Orson ever watched it, but he publicly commented on Hank's work on the film years later: "The music, which I didn't have anything to do with, was, I thought, quite well done. I think he did a fine job," Welles said. Hank began to shop tapes of his *Touch of Evil* score to record labels to be released as a Latin jazz album. Decca Records passed on it, but a small label called Challenge Records signed him and suddenly Hank had his first soundtrack album of a dramatic score released in the summer of 1959.

The twins were about to turn four and Chris was an energetic six-year-old. Ginny was beginning to take sessions again here and there, whenever she could get a babysitter. They celebrated the Challenge record deal with an expensive bottle of red wine they'd been saving for a special occasion. But they were toasting to more than just that one deal; Hank had learned what would take others practicing the craft of scoring for motion pictures a lifetime to learn. It was a path that would soon disappear out from under him, however, and one that would no longer be there for those who followed, due to the collapse of the studio system. By the late '50s, the methods of filmmaking were already becoming old fashioned and the equipment ancient. They were years of decline, in which television became more popular than going to the movies.

"Challenge was smart to pick up the *Touch of Evil* soundtrack. I think it will be a tremendous success," Ginny said, raising her glass.

"From your lips to God's ears, darling," Hank said as he looked over at their three little ones. The twins were already figuring out that they could trick their daddy into not being able to tell them apart. They giggled every time he fell for it.

"I'm lucky Joe allowed me to put that band together and record when I did," Hank said. "The recording studio at Universal is falling apart. They're not staying up to date with the latest techniques in film production and music recording, as much as I've tried to get them to invest in some new gear. The record companies are so far ahead with new recording techniques, getting that fuller, more modern sound."

Television had also surpassed films in popularity and was able to take the lead by investing in lots of new equipment. There were also more and more movies being made by outside production companies as a result of the *United States v. Paramount Pictures* decision, which made it illegal for studios to own theaters, thereby ending the studio system. Hank would soon use this to his advantage after 1958, when Universal made the decision to let go of their staff of film composers—a few days before he needed a haircut.

Chapter Eight

FIFTY-TWO MILES

Despite no longer being employed by Universal, Hank retained the pass that allowed him to drive onto the Universal lot. The guards who manned the studio gates had gotten to know him over the past six years and considered him a fine friend who would ask about their families and their lives. He'd likely earned lifetime privileges to get on the lot, pass or no pass.

The first sign that it was all coming to an end was when the Universal orchestra's contract was not renewed. The orchestra was a big expense for the studio, and combined with the staff composer salaries—a lot of money back then, at $300 to $400 a week—it all added up to a big outlay of cash that was no longer making financial sense. Universal was in a very different position than its neighbor, Warner Brothers, which had been investing heavily in the new medium of television. When Hank was officially notified that the studio was letting go of its staff composers, he'd been working on the James Cagney picture *Never Steal Anything Small,* which would be his last under his staff composer contract—but not nearly his last for the studio, though he didn't know that yet. He always knew this job, which was almost too good to be true, was not going to last forever, but it was incredibly bittersweet to see it come to an end. The music department had become a close-knit unit and Hank felt forever indebted to Joe Gershenson and Milt Rosen for giving him his shot at breaking into the business. Hank would miss the camaraderie of working somewhere that felt like a home away from home, which was important to him if he was going to have to spend so many hours at work.

During Hank's six years at Universal, he'd worked with certain directors multiple times. One of these was Blake Edwards, who'd been a friend of Ginny going back to when they ran in the same social circles as young adults. One day not too long after finishing out his contract, Hank needed a haircut and figured he would make an afternoon of it and go to Universal to have lunch at the commissary and pop into the barbershop. Strolling down one of the picture-perfect sidewalks of the backlot—the outdoor areas used for shooting exterior scenes—Hank was already feeling nostalgic about his days at the dream factory. He marveled at how one side of the street resembled a big city street, and the other side Middle America. He smiled to himself and headed into the barbershop.

"Good afternoon," he greeted everyone inside.

"Why, hello, Hank!" one of the barbers said, motioning for him to have a seat in his chair.

The barber wrapped him in a cape as Hank joked, "Seems I can't stay away from this place."

"It's not going to be the same without all you music people around here. You guys have the best stories! Now where am I going to get my material?"

Hank chuckled. "Gee, now that I've lost my job, I'm hoping all my hair doesn't fall out."

"Promise you'll come back even if it does?"

"You bet. Did I ever tell you my Italian mother's advice?"

"What was that?"

"She'd tell me to rub olive oil on my head for a nice, thick head of hair."

"Is that so?"

"Yes. But even Italian mothers can be wrong," Hank laughed.

The barber took care of Hank, who tipped him handsomely, just as his first mentor Max Adkins had taught him.

Then he stepped outside in the bright light of day and ran into Blake Edwards.

"Hank!"

"Hi, Blake!"

They pumped hands enthusiastically.

"How's everything? How is Ginny?" Blake asked.

"Aside from having her hands full with three kids, just great."

"Please give her my best, will you?"

"Of course."

"Listen, Hank, I'm shooting a new television show. We just came out of a meeting about it." Blake pointed across the way. "There's Don Sharpe over there, who'll be producing. He did *I Love Lucy*. Procter & Gamble is lined up as the sponsor, so we already have the go-ahead for thirteen episodes. You think you might be interested in doing music for us?"

"Is it already getting around that I'm unemployed?" Hank joked. "Of course I'm interested!"

At the time, Blake was thirty-eight and Hank was thirty-six. Blake wanted a partner who was his contemporary—a young guy on his way up who would bring something fresh to project.

"The show is called *Peter Gunn.*"

"That's great. I've always wanted to do a Western."

Blake laughed. "I'll have a script sent over to you. Call me once you've read it."

Hank chuckled as he flipped over the last page of the teleplay while sitting in the living room at home. "This is not a Western!"

"Oh, no?" Ginny asked.

"Peter Gunn is a private investigator who loves jazz and hangs out in a jazz roadhouse called Mother's, where his love interest is the singer."

"Well, that sounds exciting."

"I'd say the score had better be jazzy, then, wouldn't you?"

"Oh, yes! How fun."

Hank went to the piano. "I'm hearing kind of that walking bass and drums. You know, the West Coast jazz kind of sound."

"I love that."

As he began noodling around on the keys, an idea came to him rather suddenly. "Hey! What about guitar and piano playing together, ostinato?"

"Oh, I forgot to tell you that your father called."

Hank started laughing almost uncontrollably.

"What is so funny?" Ginny asked.

"Just that 'ostinato' made you think of my father."

She started laughing along with him because *ostinato* means *obstinate.* "Oh, gosh, did I really just do that?"

"Yes, you did," Hank said, laughing almost uncontrollably.

Hank would call his father back before it got too late, but he felt like he might already be on to something.

"I think maybe the ostinato should be sustained throughout

the piece to give it a kind of sinister effect." Hank got more and more excited as the music began erupting out of him. "And how about some frightened saxophones and shouting brass?"

"I'm not sure I've ever heard frightened saxophones. Or shouting brass, for that matter!"

Ginny loved to watch Hank work, especially when ideas were literally pouring out of him. She'd felt some concern when she first learned he was going to be out of a job. Hank could sense she was troubled by the thought of them having no money with kids to raise. This welcome news lightened her mood and she couldn't help but glow with pride.

"When one door closes, another one opens," she said.

It seemed that Hank couldn't have stumbled onto a better project to work on. He was juiced and oozing with clear-eyed creativity.

Hank soon learned that his budget to record the *Peter Gunn* theme was only going to cover an eleven-piece orchestra. This meant he would have to get inventive with the instrumentation. He worked feverishly developing his concept for the theme and the show's sound and, in the process, his deep affinity for flutes became clear. Not only did they have a special place in his heart as the first instrument he learned to play, but he was beginning to hear things he could do with flutes that had never been done before. *Peter Gunn* would be the first score with an entire section of bass flutes, which surprised Ginny, who was quite knowledgeable about music.

"An entire *section* of them? I can't even imagine what that's going to sound like! What is it you call them?" she asked him.

"The plumber's nightmare," he said wryly. This nickname described the hairpin curves of the bass flute, an instrument that was virtually undiscovered in film scores.

She laughed. "You are so silly."

"I didn't come up with that one. Wish I had, though."

Hank lifted up one of the twins to wipe her face.

"I'm going to have to move away from all the old string tremolo business," he said. "The large orchestra playing all the time is outmoded anyway. The bass flute has such a wonderful gloomy, ominous quality. There's nothing else like it."

Hank would soon come to find out that there was one problem with bass flutes, which was that there weren't that many of them around. But that didn't stop him from insisting on them. The Mancini recording orchestra would come to call for piccolos, flutes, alto flutes, and bass flutes. With this palette of sounds, Hank was able to develop his own musical vocabulary. He had an instinct that would later be proven true—that the sparseness of the sound he was creating for the *Peter Gunn* theme would be new and novel, and that the stripped-down instrumentation would be exactly what would catch people's ears by breaking through everything else that sounded so lush and full. The leaner ensemble also forced him to find new ways of creating tension and suspense. Hank turned everything on its head by asking a new question, one that was antithetical to the way film composers had normally approached things: How could he make the best use not of the *largest* studio orchestra, but of the bare minimum? Necessity as the mother of invention forced him into this realization and led the way to a shocking success.

At this point in film composing, the process involved writing out every part for every instrument—keeping melody, harmony, rhythm, and sub-melody bar by bar. By the time it was all said and done, Hank had written *fifty-two miles* of score for the *Peter Gunn* theme. Once the pilot episode was finished and the theme recorded, a shrewd executive at NBC got the idea to put out the soundtrack on a record album and a meeting was set up for Hank with RCA Records, who had a contract with Hank's friend and fine trumpet player, Shorty Rogers. Shorty and drummer Shelly Manne were both part of the West Coast jazz movement, which represented a more relaxed style that reflected the mood and rhythms of California more than the hard bebop and edge of New York. Shorty and Shelly played on the 1955 Elmer Bernstein's jazz soundtrack for the Frank Sinatra film *The Man with the Golden Arm*, which Hank thought was sharp and arresting. Hank knew Shorty had a guaranteed sale of eighty thousand albums, which was huge for jazz, and the label initially thought Shorty should be the artist to record the *Peter Gunn* soundtrack. Hank and Shorty met to talk it over.

"This tune is really something, Hank."

"You like it? So, you'll record it?"

"Hank, I have no reason to record this. You wrote it, you arranged it, and *you* should record it."

Hank was dumbfounded. "But, Shorty, I'm not exactly a recording artist. Nobody knows who I am. You have a name."

"Hank, get serious, man. I'm not recording your song. You are."

Shorty was immoveable. He called the song Hank's "baby." Shorty didn't know it then, but he would be doing Hank an incredible service by insisting on this.

With their entire focus on sound, record companies had been much more astute in using jazz players and musicians fresh off the road from dance bands on their recordings. This was not the case with the film studios, who tended to use jazz musicians only with great reluctance and only if the score specifically called for jazz. Hank had been able to pave the way a bit with the band he assembled for the *Touch of Evil* soundtrack and now, once again, he was going to be using all musicians from outside the film studio circle. The other major misconception the studios had about jazz players was that they couldn't read music and would be lost when faced with a classical piece. The opposite was actually true—classical pieces were the easiest for these incredible musicians, as they could read and play anything. Most of the musicians Hank hired for the *Peter Gunn* sessions had formerly been with all the top bands and were incredible soloists in their own right. Hank knew these qualities were what would bring out the greatest amount of dimension and depth in the music. The recording sessions for *Peter Gunn* would give him many opportunities to show what a maverick he was.

As Hank had been lamenting for a while, the recording facilities on the Universal lot were incredibly lacking. He knew it would be a challenge to get a good sound out of them—good enough to capture the brilliance of the players he was hiring. Getting the right people was only part of the equation. It wouldn't matter if they weren't recorded properly. This was 1958 and the recording engineers on the film lots still thought in terms of a single mic hung over the orchestra. Hank wanted people to be aware of all the musical detail in the score, so he borrowed from record company techniques that were achieving a much more complex and exciting sound. It would take the film studios years to catch up, but Hank was doing his part to bridge these two worlds. In doing so, he was able to bring the studios into the current times and create more job opportunities for musicians.

When the day of the session arrived, Hank asked the Universal recording engineers for a microphone on the drums, one on the piano, and another on the bass. Although they looked at him as though he were an alien with two heads, they did as he asked—and it was a good thing too. *Peter Gunn* went on the air in September 1958 with the first jazz score in television history. It was unprecedented to have a television score put out on an album. Not having any model from which to gauge the demand, RCA pressed only eight thousand copies. They sold out in the first week. Hank had not felt he was being given the best treatment by RCA when he first heard that relatively low number—a fraction of what they would have done if it had been put out under Shorty Rogers. He returned home one day to tell Ginny what was happening and to remind her that RCA had also foolishly signed Hank to only a one-album deal.

"All hell is breaking loose," he said. "They're running around like madmen at RCA, trying to keep up with the demand."

Ginny threw her arms around him. "I'm so happy for you, darling."

"I suppose they should have done a bigger initial pressing."

"Now that's your job too, is it?"

Given that *The Music from Peter Gunn* was released under Henry Mancini's name, it made him a public and very successful recording artist overnight. The album went to number one on the Billboard chart and stayed there for ten weeks. It dropped slightly after that but stayed on the charts for another 117 weeks and sold over a million copies, which was unprecedented for *any* jazz album at that time. As production on the television show went on, Hank was busy breaking more new ground by scoring each individual episode, instead of relying on music editors to cut different pieces together. What made the real difference were all the amazing soloists who brought a unique quality to the music and provided a punch that drove each episode, just as Hank had hoped. One of these musicians was a pianist named John Williams, who went on to compose the music for *Star Wars*.

Peter Gunn was Hank's first major step toward completely

remaking film and television music. His was a truly distinctive style in the making that was moving the sonic landscape out of the nineteenth century and into the twentieth. The Mancini sound marked a major shift away from the European symphonic style to a crisper, modern mode that was tailor-made for a rapidly changing America and the baby boomer generation. He was breezing into the next decade, shaping it as he went in a way that perfectly reflected the culture around him. And, once again, Hank's timing was impeccable—the very first Grammy Awards were going to be held on May 4, 1959. The music from *Peter Gunn* was named Album of the Year, beating not one but *two* albums from Frank Sinatra, *Ella Fitzgerald Sings the Irving Berlin Songbook*, and Van Cliburn's recording of a Tchaikovsky concerto.

Blake Edwards was appropriately generous in his public proclamations crediting fifty percent of *Peter Gunn*'s success to Hank's music. In interviews, he loved to tell the story of the first time he heard the theme song. "I just about fell down," he said. "I was absolutely gobsmacked. There's no two ways about it. I knew I'd chosen the right guy to do the music."

The two of them made great partners and Edwards was wise to share the acclaim, as it was just the beginning of a long and fruitful partnership. It also occurred to Hank that this was the first time he wouldn't be writing for a major studio, but rather Blake's independent production company. If there was one thing he'd learned in life, and specifically in this industry, it's that you don't get what you don't ask for. He approached Blake one day with a request.

"Blake, would you consider allowing me to keep my own copyrights?" he asked.

"Sure, Hank. Why not?"

There was potentially a big reason why not, but Blake was a generous partner and was truly grateful that Hank's music was serving Blake's own work so well. He could have easily said that he wanted to retain the copyrights of the music for his company, which was standard practice. But he saw more value in keeping his partner happy and making sure he knew how much he was appreciated. Blake may have not known it at the time, but he was setting a precedent, as this was the first time a composer was allowed to keep the copyrights to his or her own music. The fact that *Peter Gunn* ended up being a hit television series meant that the lion's share of the profits were going back to Hank. The norm had always been for the studios to essentially extort this money from the composers who created the work, so that for any reuse or future use the studio would retain fifty percent of the publishing royalties. From that point on, Hank asked for ownership of his copyrights in all of his contracts. He wouldn't always get it, and he wouldn't let it be a deal breaker if the project was important to him, but he was gaining more and more leverage all the time. When CBS approached Blake Edwards to do another series, they insisted that the music of Henry Mancini be in the contract. After many years, Hank's first royalty check for "The Soft-Shoe Boogie" for $14.73 arrived in the mail. Hank had it framed where he could always see it when he was working, as a reminder of how far he'd come.

Hank arrived home one afternoon to find boxes piled high on the front porch. Ginny opened the front door.

"I've already carried about a dozen of them inside already," she told him.

"What's in them?"

"Fan mail for *Peter Gunn*."

"Doesn't that usually go to the studio?" he asked.

"They're the ones who sent it all over. It's not for the show. Every single one of these is about the song!"

Hank was receiving more fan mail than the show itself! He and Ginny had great fun reading people's letters.

"This one says, 'Your music inspired me to learn an instrument at thirty-nine years old just so I could play the theme from *Peter Gunn* for my friends.'"

"This one's from a high school student who said he joined his marching band," Hank said. "'I began listening to a lot more jazz after hearing your brilliant masterpiece from *Peter Gunn*,'" Hank read aloud. "'Brilliant masterpiece.' I like that."

Despite most people referring to "Peter Gunn" as jazz, Hank would always contend that the theme was derived more from rock and roll. *Peter Gunn* aired on Monday nights and all the kids in the neighborhood got a big kick out of the fact that the composer of that instantly iconic piece of music lived on their street. The twins, about eight years old, were doing their part, selling the albums out in front of the Mancini house for a quarter a piece. They were still too young to appreciate the math involved—Hank had purchased them from the label for a dollar each, but he sure did appreciate their enthusiasm.

Never one to rest on his laurels, Hank was feeling confident there would more work for him on the horizon. He and Ginny had been talking for a while about doing a little traveling as soon as he could carve out the time. When they'd reached their goal of saving up $6,000 for a trip, they flew to New York, where they embarked on one of the last Atlantic crossings aboard the *Liberté*. Once in Europe, they spent six weeks on the continent with RCA people, who took them to all the best places in Europe's capital cities. This treatment was a far cry from Hank's initial dealings with the label, which was regretting its decision to sign him only to one album. This put Hank in a much stronger negotiating position when RCA decided it wanted to do another album of *More Music from Peter Gunn*.

When Hank and Ginny returned home, Ginny had to begin rehearsals right away for a benefit show in which she was performing. Hank's heart sank when he went to the bank and found out there was less than $5 left in their account after the trip. He went home and started working when the mail arrived. Walking to the mailbox, filled with his usual dread about bills and money, he opened one of the envelopes and his mouth fell open. It was the first royalty check for *Peter Gunn*—for $32,000. Completely stunned, he handled it like a stick of lit dynamite and drove straight to the Coconut Grove, where Ginny was rehearsing. He handed it to her. Her eyes welled up with tears.

"What d'ya think would have happened if I hadn't needed a haircut that day?" he asked her.

Chapter Nine

HUCKLEBERRY FRIEND

Hank allowed himself to take a deep breath of relief after receiving the first installment of "mailbox money," as residual earners affectionately refer to it. He had no way of knowing just *how much* money would be at stake when he asked Blake to consider letting him keep 100 percent of his own copyrights—he could only hope it would be significant and be the beginning of building a catalog of music that would continue to earn for his family long after he was gone. He felt absolute gratitude toward Shorty Rogers for urging him so strongly to record his own song. If Shorty had recorded and released "Peter Gunn" for RCA, a good deal of this money would have been in his mailbox instead of Hank's.

Hank was learning so much from all the people who were coming into his orbit and was thankful for each and every one of them. He learned not take it personally when he found anyone's treatment of him lacking, like the way RCA handled his recording contract by setting expectations so low. Instead, he made a conscious effort to learn something from every experience and not get bogged down with negativity when things did not go his way. He quickly learned he would be the one to benefit in the end when he trusted in the process, which was mysterious. He was earning the respect of everyone in the industry—not only for his talent, but for his integrity. The trip to Europe had recharged his batteries and inspired him creatively, and now, with some financial cushion, he was ready to confidently face the future.

Hank started to believe one should never trust "this thing called success," he'd say, and he lived accordingly. Part of this meant learning how to juggle projects. During the first season of *Peter Gunn*, he took on a film starring Tony Curtis called *The Great Impostor* about the real life charlatan Ferdinand W. Demara Jr. The film was well received and brought him more attention as a composer. Hank's next film, *High Time*, would be directed by his friend Blake Edwards and would star Bing Crosby. The picture would showcase Bing Crosby's crooning with the song "The Second Time Around" in a poignant scene in which his character's wife overhears the touching lyrics from another room in the house and is moved to tears. Written by the power team of Sammy Cahn and Jimmy Van Heusen, Hank and his orchestra would be the first to record it.

Hank went into *High Time* having heard about Bing Crosby's tendency to be aloof and dismissive. As always, he kept an open mind and his personal experience with Bing turned out to be enjoyable. Perhaps Bing extended Hank a warmth he didn't show everyone, because of their shared interest in pipe smoking. During a rehearsal early on, Hank noticed Bing's unusually thin-stemmed pipe, which seemed to be a permanent fixture.

"Say, Bing, what kind of pipe is that?" Hank asked.

"This here's a Merchant Service pipe. I pick them up in a shop over in London."

"Ah, very exotic," Hank smiled.

Bing reached into his bag and pulled out an extra one. "Here, take this one," he said.

"Oh, no, you don't have to do that."

"Nonsense. I stock up on them when I'm over there for this very reason."

"Really?"

"Yes, I insist."

"Thank you kindly," Hank said. "I'll have to find that shop next time I'm over there."

Hank was staying extremely busy with another season of *Peter Gunn*, as well as with a second television series of Blake Edwards's called *Mr. Lucky*, loosely based on the 1943 film starring Cary Grant. The eponymous character on the not-so-lucky television show was a suave don who ran a gambling ship off the coast of California. CBS began to receive innumerable complaints from religious fundamentalists about the gaming portrayed on the show and forced Edwards to turn Mr. Lucky's den of iniquity into a restaurant. Ratings slipped precipitously. One critic cheekily wrote, "The millions of corrupt Americans who had liked the show turned to other stations." The series was cancelled after only one season, but it was just enough time for Hank to score another number-one hit. The theme from Mr. Lucky led to recording an entire album of music from the show and Hank started to use "Mr. Lucky" as a nickname for himself.

RCA now wanted more jazz-pop albums from Hank, whether or not they were tied into a film or television series. In the summer of 1959, he recorded a new album of standards from the big-band era called *The Mancini Touch*. The project took advantage of all the amazing players Hank had been using in his television and film scores, including pianist John Williams and drummer Shelly Manne. Hank's orchestrations for this album were exquisite—atmospheric, original, and refreshing—all sweetened by RCA's new high-fidelity stereo recording process. The RCA engineers knew how to best capture the sound of the Mancini players by close-miking each one individually and then remixing them back together for the home stereo speaker system. The new technology allowed Hank's unique style of orchestration to ring through crisply and become immediately identifiable. One of his signature sounds became French horns playing the top of chords over trombones with sustained pads set against the melody. Over and over again, his unique understanding of flutes continued to come into play. He'd use high piccolos in unison with the lead line on string passages, which gave the strings what could be described as an icy sound. No other film composer at the time had Hank's moody and affecting style of string writing.

Unaware of the far-reaching aspects of what he was doing at the time, Hank was almost singlehandedly bringing a fresh sound to film scoring in the late 1950s. This is not to say there had not been any jazz in film before Hank began doing it. His friend and West Coast jazzer Bud Shank wrote a jazz score for the surf film *Slippery When Wet* in 1959. Johnny Mandel and others with jazz backgrounds were getting into film scoring too, but Mandel said he felt it was Hank who made jazz so widely accepted in film scoring by proving how successful and expressive it could be. What was most astonishing about Hank's rise was his level of modesty, which was in lockstep with his success. Musicians loved Hank because he was a joy to work with and he was creating more opportunities for session players. They'd always leave his sessions feeling uplifted and appreciated—Hank made sure of that. No one ever turned down a chance to work with him because they knew what they'd be missing.

It was around this time that Hank also began to also make it his business to give back, especially to the next generation of composers. He knew that those coming up would be doing it without the benefit of any kind of apprenticeship like he'd had at Universal. This meant there would be a great need to codify and share his knowledge of orchestration. Hank was in the position of being able to use all his RCA recordings, so he decided to publish a book on the subject—*Sounds and Scores: A Practical Guide to Professional Orchestration*—in order to provide actual examples that showed how various combinations of instruments sounded while reading along with the written scores, just the way he'd taught himself to do at Juilliard. Many instruments in the orchestra are referred to as transposing instruments, so a score will be written in different keys for them. For example, a notated middle C on a transposing instrument produces a pitch other than middle C, such as with a B-flat clarinet, which sounds a concert B-flat. Transposing instruments do not sound in different keys—they sound in what is called concert pitch. Part of *Sounds and Scores* also reassembled Mancini scores *in concert* to make it possible for someone not yet skilled in transposition to study them. To this day, it remains one of the most widely used texts in orchestration courses.

By 1961, Blake Edwards was ready to make a move from television to film. A novella written by Truman Capote called *Breakfast at Tiffany's* caught his attention. Blake's initial creative decision was to set the screen adaptation in the 1960s, instead of the 1940s, as the book was. Capote lobbied aggressively to cast Marilyn Monroe in the part of Holly Golightly, but it was a Paramount film and Marilyn was still under contract at Twentieth Century Fox at the time. After considering several actresses, Paramount cast Audrey Hepburn. By now, Hank was considered part of a package deal with Blake. In their early discussions, they tried to figure out how best to evoke Manhattan in the film.

"Why does every single film about New York have to revert to Gershwin?" Blake wondered.

"That's a great question, Blake. But we're not going to do that, so not to worry."

"So, how *will* we evoke that special, singular feeling about New York being at the heart of so many people's dreams?"

"If we just take our cues from the character of Holly, we can't go wrong," Hank said. "She makes me think of a combination of warm-sounding strings, with vibes as the percussion, and that street-corner sax sound. The music has got to celebrate the sophisticated party culture, while at the same time capture the yearning of Holly and all who go to New York searching for something," Hank said.

"You sound like you have a pretty good handle on it already," Blake said.

Hank smiled.

"The other thing we need to discuss is the song. The producers have already been talking about dubbing Audrey with a singer." Blake was referring to producers Marty Jurow and Richard Shepherd.

"You mean she can't sing at all?" Hank said.

"She's done some singing, sure, but . . ."

Hank could tell Blake was a little worried about how to pull this off.

"But dubbing her might be riskier than letting her sing it with that lovely voice of hers. Who else sounds like that?" Hank asked.

"No one."

"Right."

"It's a moment that has the potential to make or break the film."

"Then, we'll make sure it *makes* it," Hank said. He flipped the script open to the scene, where he'd already made lots of notes. "So, she's on the fire escape. Think about that. Fire *escape*. As a viewer, shouldn't we also be involved in a bit of escape? It's that yearning I was talking about."

"Are you saying you want to write the song as well as the score?"

"Well, I sure would like a crack at it."

"It might take an act of congress to change Marty's and Dick's minds. They're convinced we need to bring in a Broadway songwriter. They don't see you as a melodist, Hank. You know I couldn't disagree with them more on this."

"Don't they know I was nominated for *The Glenn Miller Story*?"

"Probably not."

Hank chuckled. "Well, maybe I'll just start working up some ideas."

"Yes, you must. And I'll go to work on those two," Blake said.

Hank's agent, Henry Alper, also wanted to play it safe.

"Hank, you have a hell of a picture here with a great director and a great star—don't rock the boat. Let someone else do the song; you do the score," he said.

These would become famous last words that Hank thankfully did not heed. After some haggling, Blake was able to convince the producers that Hank should at the very least be given a chance to write the song. Hank felt somewhat vindicated, but given the opportunity, he couldn't think of anything! Mellifluous as Audrey's voice was, she had a very limited range.

Then, one night, perhaps not coincidentally, Hank and Ginny were watching television when the film *Funny Face* starring Audrey and Fred Astaire came on. They watched her perform the Gershwin tune "How Long Has This Been Going On?"

"Her voice is lovely, dear," Ginny said. "It has such a delicate breathiness and a very nice vibrato."

"Yes, but what is that range? About an octave and a half?"

Hank went to the piano and played it. An octave and a half it was.

"Okay, well. I've got my work cut out for me," he said.

The next morning, Hank began playing around with a three-note fragment in the key of C. But weeks went by and he still had not landed on a melody. Then, one day, it hit him like a lightning bolt. As he would later say, it took him "a month and thirty minutes to write" what would become known as "Moon River." He played it for Ginny first, as he always did with something new. When he finished the song and she clutched at her heart, he knew he had a winner. He loved the simplicity of it and that it was completely diatonic, meaning it could be played on only white piano keys. Once again, it was the notion of constraints, just as he had to contend with on *Peter Gunn*, that had brought forth enormous creativity.

For the lyrics, Hank wanted the best. He'd first met Johnny

Mercer after Johnny put words to "Joanna," an instrumental piece from the second *Peter Gunn* album. Nothing ever came of it, but from that point on they'd always wanted to work together. Many of his peers considered Mercer quite possibly the best American lyricist ever. His range included wit and humor, evocative blues, and everything in between. Another legendary songwriter of the time, Sammy Cahn, said, "Mercer was no poet. Shakespeare was a poet. But Shakespeare was no Johnny Mercer!" Johnny had been writing songs since he was twenty-three with earlier legends such as Hoagy Carmichael. Like Hank, he'd also worked with the King of Swing, Benny Goodman, writing the iconic "Hooray for Hollywood" for the film *Hollywood Hotel*, which starred Goodman.

Except now, Johnny was at a low point in his career and had long been known to be a melancholic.

"Rock and roll has taken over the music business, Hank. You know that," Johnny said when Hank first played him the song to see if he wanted to work together on it.

"It's very pretty, Hank. Beautiful. But I have to tell you, I don't know if I'm the right guy to write a lyric for you. If I'm being honest, my career is over."

"Johnny, that's nonsense. Truly."

"I fear the time has passed for my kind of lyrics and your kind of music," Johnny said.

"What if I told you not to worry about any of that and just write me something?"

"I'd say fine, but who is going to record a waltz ten years into rock and roll?"

"I just told you not to worry about that."

"Oh, right."

"It feels right for this. You've got to trust me."

Johnny kind of shook his head in disbelief. "It does, yes. I suppose we'll just write it for the film and that will be that. It won't have any commercial appeal."

"Okay, Johnny. I look forward to hearing what you come up with."

Hank's process with Johnny became much like Blake's process with Hank. Blake and Hank would reach an understanding of what the music should to be, then Hank would go off to write and Blake wouldn't hear anything until it was time to record. Hank took the same tact with Johnny: he'd hand over the music and Johnny would come back with three different sets of lyrics. When Johnny was ready to show Hank what he'd written for his *Breakfast at Tiffany's* waltz, Hank was conducting his orchestra for a benefit at the Beverly Wilshire and asked to meet him at the hotel. There they found a deserted ballroom with a piano. Johnny played the first set of lyrics he'd come up with, which began with, "I'm Holly."

"I don't know about that one," Johnny said.

"Let's hear the next one," Hank said as he began to play the song from the beginning again.

Johnny sang through his second set of lyrics, which were quite different from the first. As soon as Johnny began to croon "Mooooon river, " Hank felt chills. When Johnny sang "my huckleberry friend," Hank could feel the hair on the back of his neck stand on end. It was the incredible rush of knowing they'd just hit on pure magic. It sent a jolt through Hank's heart.

"John. Wow."

"You like that one?"

"Yes. That's the one. I've never been more sure of anything in my life."

"Well, great."

Both of them took a minute to let it sink in.

"Now, what in the world is a huckleberry?"

Johnny laughed. "Oh, it might as well be a blueberry. You'd never even know the difference. You know how Southerners have funny names for things," he kidded.

"I just love how the river feels like a metaphor for life, with its surface flow and unknown depths," Hank said.

In Hank's mind, the lyrics for "Moon River" went beyond perfection and captured the wistful longing of Holly Golightly and the generation she represented. At the same time, the folk quality of it had tapped into Mercer's Southern roots, and Blake and the producers loved it. Hank's idea to use harmonica as solo instrumentation against the lonely image and delicate beauty of Audrey Hepburn gazing through the windows of Tiffany & Co. was seen as contrasting and brilliant. Hank pre-recorded the song with Audrey so that she could play the ukulele and sing along during the filming of the scene. Hank then went on to compose his dazzling score for *Breakfast at Tiffany's*. Once a cut of the film was complete, Hank received a letter from Audrey:

Dear Henry,

I have just seen our picture—BREAKFAST AT TIFFANY'S—this time with your score.

A movie without music is a little bit like an aeroplane without fuel. However beautifully the job is done, we are still on the ground and in a world of reality. Your music has lifted us all up and sent us soaring. Everything we cannot say with words or show with action you have expressed for us. You have done this with so much imagination, fun and beauty.

You are the hippest of cats—and most sensitive of composers!

Thank you, dear Hank.

Lots of love,
Audrey

A preview screening of the film was organized for an audience in San Francisco. A whole group attended to see how it would play—Blake, Hank and Ginny, Audrey and husband Mel Ferrer, Dick and Marty, and the head of Paramount Studios, Marty Rackin. The screening went incredibly well even though they agreed that the film was running long and some cuts were needed. Everyone thought the "Moon River" scene and song played very well, and Blake was the most excited of anyone. They returned to the hotel and convened in Marty Rackin's suite to exchange thoughts and lobby for their own interests. Leaning on the fireplace mantel, Rackin looked at everyone and delivered his opening salvo as though it was the most obvious thing in the world.

"Well, the song has to go," he said.

Hank looked over at Blake, who was livid. Audrey's cherubic face also looked murderous. The song was not going without a fight from them. Hank would look back years later and wonder how so many people could have been *so* wrong. First, there was

Hank's agent, who thought he should leave well enough alone and let someone else write the song. Then there was Johnny Mercer's prediction that the song would have no commercial appeal (it went on to be recorded over one thousand times, and he was never happier to be proven wrong that the kids would reject the waltz in the age of rock and roll). Then there was the final insult of the head of Paramount Studios demanding the song be cut from the film. For the boomers, *Breakfast at Tiffany's* and Hank's music seemed to embody their hopes and aspirations without sacrificing any honest sentiment by going too far with the need to be cool.

By this time, Hank had bought a boat to take the family out on Sundays. He'd purchased it from the production of *Mr. Lucky* when it wrapped. It was the boat from the show that was used to shuttle patrons back and forth to the gambling ship. He got it for a very good price, renamed it the *Gunn Boat*, and kept her in a slip in Newport Beach. One weekend while out on a sail with Ginny and the kids, they passed another boat of one of Hank's Paramount colleagues, who raised his glass and shouted across the channel, "Aren't you glad you practiced, Hank?"

Chapter Ten

CRESCENDO

Once again, the early morning hours of winter proved fortuitous for Hank when the phone rang before dawn. It was the Academy calling. He doubted his own ears for a moment as the calm voice on the other end of the line informed him he'd been nominated for not just one Oscar, but for *three*. And there was another twist—he would be competing against himself in the category of Best Song because he and Johnny were up for "Moon River" and Hank was also nominated for his song "Bachelor in Paradise," from the film of the same name. There had been some talk around town that "Moon River" could possibly score a nomination, but the other one came as a complete surprise.

The third nomination, for Best Score, was by far the most meaningful for Hank. Becoming a film composer was what he'd always dreamed of and suddenly he was being singled out as one of the best in the world. On the other hand, he didn't consider himself a songwriter in the truest sense of the word—he just happened to possess that elusive gift for melody, which not every composer had. He viewed his own process as one in which he wrote themes that could be adapted all kinds of ways, including having lyrics added by a collaborator. Even in the case of *Breakfast at Tiffany's*, the melody of "Moon River" was Holly Golightly's theme as much as it was a stand-alone song. Despite Hank's own dubious self-assessment of his songwriting skills, one reporter put it this way: "As a songwriter, Mancini has the gift—without equal among his contemporaries—of creating melodies that have a simplicity, a directness, and inevitable flow that it's impossible not to believe you haven't heard it before." Indeed, most everyone agreed that "Moon River," as well as "Peter Gunn," had the quality of piercing the memory as if it had been there for years. Hank was the last person able to provide an explanation for this. "I don't know where those melodies come from," he said. But he was thankful that they did.

He and Ginny picked up a copy of *The Hollywood Reporter* to read the full list of nominations. Seeing his name in print next to the other nominees for Best Score sent shockwaves of excitement and terror through him. The names belonged to composers Hank grew up idolizing: Dimitri Tiomkin was nominated for *The Guns of Navarone*, Miklós Rózsa was up for *El Cid*, Elmer Bernstein for *Summer and Smoke*, and Morris Stoloff and Harry Sukman for *Fanny*. Hank was filled with equal parts delight and disbelief.

"This doesn't feel quite real," he said in a low voice to Ginny, unable to take his eyes off of the paper.

"I wish I could say I'm as shocked as you are," she smiled. "But I'm not one bit surprised."

He finally looked up at her and beamed.

"Darling, I am so incredibly proud of you," she said, taking his hands in hers. "You have worked so hard and you truly deserve this."

"I'm going to enjoy it while I can. I mean, there's no chance of beating a bench like that."

Ginny had to bite her lip as Hank continued to express the thoughts running through his mind.

"But, you know, this could lead to more important films, which could mean more nominations," he said. "Then maybe, down the road, I might win one."

"You just might," she said with a wink and smile.

"I can barely feel my head on top of my shoulders right now." He started laughing.

"In any case, let's do the Oscars right. We'll rent a limousine to pick us up and then swing over to get Johnny and Ginger on the way."

"That sounds great," he said.

"Wonderful. I'll phone Ginger, and she and I can work out all the details."

On April 9, 1962, Hank and Ginny dressed in their finery and went to pick up the Mercers, who had a lovely yet modest-sized home, given Johnny's outsized career and accomplishments. It was right on the Bel-Air Country Club golf course, situated in one of the canyons north of Sunset Boulevard. Johnny had a small studio in the back where he worked, typing out his lyrics on a typewriter; he'd been a champion typist growing up. They drank champagne on their way to the Santa Monica Civic Auditorium, where the ceremony was held then. The auditorium didn't have the grandeur of the Pantages Theatre, which evoked old Hollywood and was where Hank and Ginny had attended the Oscars seven years earlier for their first time, when he was nominated for *The Glenn Miller Story*. But this was the new

Hollywood—the industry was changing and the Academy was growing, reflected in the 2,500 voting members who cast ballots for that year's awards. Riding in the direction of the setting sun toward the ocean, Hank tried to take it all in. In these moments, he wanted to make sure he never forgot where he'd come from. He shook his head in disbelief.

"A penny for your thoughts?" Ginny asked him.

"When I think of what it was like to come out of that little western Pennsylvania steel town in the middle of the Depression and end up here . . ." He stopped himself before getting too emotional. Then he raised his glass in a toast. "To the skinny little Italian kid from P.A., and to the poet of the mossy trees, marshes, and starry skies over Savannah."

They all raised their glasses.

"To my huckleberry friend," Johnny said.

The driver opened the limo doors and they stepped out to find themselves amongst more tuxedos and silky gowns than Hank had ever seen. People hoping to catch a glimpse of the stars had been lining up since the early morning hours angling to get a spot in the bleachers above the red carpet. As Hank glanced around, he saw Elizabeth Taylor on one side and Spencer Tracy on the other. Then Hank and his ensemble entered the auditorium and found their way to their assigned folding chairs. The auditorium was used for many different kinds of events, so there weren't permanent seats.

Hank turned to Ginny and their friends. "Are these the hardest chairs they could find?" he asked.

They giggled, which helped loosen his nerves.

"Bob Hope will be good for some laughs," Johnny said. "You'd think he'd be tired of hosting for his thirteenth time.

Should I let someone know that I'll be available for next year? People seem to forget I started out as an actor."

"I sure don't," Ginger said with a giggle.

Spirits were high and the mood inside the auditorium was jubilant. Hank looked around at all the smiling faces and thanked his lucky stars. Ginny squeezed his hand. The ceremony got underway with an announcement over the loudspeaker:

"From all over the world, wherever motion pictures are made, people who make them have gathered here for the Academy Awards program, which begins now with 'The Star-Spangled Banner' sung by Miss Mary Costa."

The audience stood for the national anthem as the opera singer and actress best known for voicing the princess Aurora in the Disney animated film *Sleeping Beauty* glided across the stage and began to sing. When she finished, the announcer's voice was heard again:

"Ladies and gentlemen, based on award-winning themes by Steiner, Newman, Rózsa, and Gold, arranged by Alexander Courage, the Oscar Fantasy 'Overture Number One,' Johnny Green conducting."

The pieces in this overture were so epic and powerful; Hank felt proud to be in the company of such esteemed talent. Many of the members of the orchestra were friends he'd worked with many times before. They sounded flawless. Conductor Johnny Green was front and center, which made it seem like a night out at a symphony performance. The music went on for five minutes or so as guests continued to fill empty seats—unlike today, where seat-fillers are hired for the express purpose of never allowing the TV audience to see an empty seat. Guests leafed through printed programs as the orchestra played. Hank's eye kept getting drawn to the neat rows of statuettes arranged on a table onstage. The Academy president introduced Bob Hope, who came out to cheerful applause.

"Good evening, ladies and gentleman, and welcome to *Judgment at Santa Monica*. Yes, here we are in Santa Monica for the real west side story."

These were topical jokes, of course, because *Judgment at Nuremburg* and *West Side Story* were up for many nominations.

Hank was filled with anticipation to see Andy Williams perform "Moon River," and he and Johnny smiled at one another as Andy began singing. Hank couldn't think of a better singer for the occasion. Earlier that year, Andy had moved from New York to Los Angeles after leaving Cadence Records to sign with Columbia. He told Hank that he was extremely honored when asked by the Academy to sing "Moon River," which he called "one of the most beautiful songs I've ever heard." Hank knew how deep Andy's emotional connection to the song was. Perhaps not coincidentally, Andy had run into Hank and Johnny a year before while they were dining at La Scala just after they'd finished the recording session with Audrey. Hank had told Andy then, "This would be a great song for you to record, Andy." He handed Andy the sheet music, which he had with him, as they'd come straight from the session—a seemingly small act that would wind up determining much of Andy's future. Andy took it back to New York and presented it to Cadence, and in yet another wrong-headed prediction about "Moon River," the head of the label didn't think the kids would respond to "huckleberry friend." It wasn't until Andy relocated to Los Angeles that the idea was fully embraced by his new label, which agreed to record the album *Moon River and Other Great Movie Themes*.

The project was recorded in three days and, having left "Moon River" for last, Andy had only ten minutes to do it. Lucky for him, he got it in one take. Hank looked on as Andy finished the song for the Oscars audience in the room and at home watching, knowing that Andy must have been feeling very good about his performance.

In another full-circle moment for Hank, Tony Martin took the stage with his wife, actress Cyd Charisse, to present the award for Best Score. Tony had been in Hank's Air Force band back at the Seymour Johnson base in North Carolina during the war, and he was one of the things about that experience that made it bearable for Hank and the other guys in the band who were miserable being stationed there. Tony and Cyd took turns reading off the nominees before Tony said, "And the winner, Cyd . . ."

She turned to receive the envelope, opened it, and, with her movie-star smile, announced, "And the winner is . . . Henry Mancini for *Breakfast at Tiffany's*."

The orchestra began to play "Moon River" as Hank stood up. He could hardly feel his legs under him. When he reached the stage, he smiled and waved at no one in particular before reaching the podium and shaking hands with his old comrade, who handed him the Oscar. His speech was about as to the point as it could be.

"I am deeply grateful to the members of the Academy and to my good friend, Blake Edwards. Thank you," he said.

Perhaps Hank the conductor didn't want to put Johnny Green in the position of playing him off.

Walking back to his seat, Hank's mind was in a state he'd never before experienced. It didn't seem to him that nearly any time had gone by before he heard his name called *again*. It was almost as though he'd forgotten about his other nominations when Debbie Reynolds came out to present the award for Best Song.

"And the Oscar for Best Song is . . ." Debbie said, "'Moon River' by Henry Mancini and Johnny Mercer."

Hank handed the Oscar he'd already won to Ginny. Johnny went running toward the stage and Hank rushed to keep up with him. Johnny deferred to Hank, who leaned into the microphone and, referring to his previous five-second speech, said, "I've already said my bit—you go ahead." Johnny leaned into the microphone.

"I'd like to say that I'm very proud you like our song. I'd like to thank you, Audrey, and thank you, Andy. And martinis for everybody."

They returned to their seats with statuettes in hand. Hank and Ginny both knew something very special was happening. They felt the air around them was somehow different. Beginning with the unexpected breakout hit with *Peter Gunn* and now with two Oscars, it felt like landing on a mountaintop. It was a night of pure joy and celebration. After the ceremony at the Academy Dinner Ball at the Hilton, Hollywood luminaries lined up to congratulate him. To be the talk of the town and to have everyone who was anyone in the business want to shake your hand and kiss your wife was quite a thrill for the normally reserved Hank. Many of his industry colleagues, though familiar with his work, had never met him in person. Many remarked on how tall Henry was.

"Just how tall are you, Hank?" one asked.

"Six-one." Then, with that droll smile, he said, "Six-two when I've got a hit."

The following day, Andy Williams' *Moon River and Other*

Great Movie Themes sold four hundred thousand copies. Andy called Hank to share his excitement.

"This goes beyond my wildest expectations," Andy told him.

"Andy, I'm so happy for you. I can't think of a better singer to bring the song to the masses."

"I have something else to thank you for as well," Andy said.

"What's that?"

"For somehow convincing my mother that *I* won an Oscar."

They laughed heartily.

"I'll see you soon. Thank you for your wonderful performance," Hank said. "I don't think any singer understands the song more or sings it better than you do."

Hank and Andy developed a deep bond forged on their similar life experiences. They were just three years apart in age and had both grown up in the heartland with very little. Andy once confided in Hank that there was a point at which he was so poor, he ate dog food to survive. Neither of them had ever forgotten their humble beginnings and they made sure to always have fun in a business known for sometimes taking itself too seriously. Oftentimes at aftershow gatherings and press events, Hank would go up to Andy and put a hand on his lower back, which is the signal from a press agent to a star to turn around and shake more hands. Andy fell for Hank's trick every time and it always made him laugh before he really did have to get out there and press the flesh.

Hank was on top of the world. It wasn't just that he had a hit—*he was* the hit. RCA, Paramount Studios, and KTLA proclaimed September 1962 Henry Mancini Month with planned events all across Los Angeles. This was the crescendo of his life and career. He'd become both the wealthiest and the most popular film composer in history, and a household name on everyone's lips. He was also the first multimedia superstar, building a bridge between the soundtrack and the baby boomer movie ticket buyers. He made the cover of *TIME* magazine, which called him "Hollywood's Hottest Music Man." Hank handled his fame in the most gracious way possible: by largely ignoring it.

Averaging three film scores per year, he and Ginny were at their peak financially and they used their power for good. With an unwavering impulse to give back, they devoted themselves to many worthy charitable causes and endowed scholarship funds for music students at UCLA and other institutions. "When life has been good to you, I think you owe something in return," Hank continued to say, and he meant it more and more each time. He got a charge out of conducting three thousand high school band members, playing his hits at the Los Angeles Coliseum. After the event, he was talking to a group of student musicians who told him how much they loved playing "Peter Gunn."

"Never has so much been made of so little," he told them.

"Mr. Mancini, how can you say that?" one of the kids asked.

"No, I just mean . . . Look, it's one chord throughout and a very simple top line."

"Yeah, but it's still so *great*."

"Thank you, son. I appreciate that. And I'm glad you enjoy playing it so much."

To think the song continues to be a marching band perennial sixty years later is beyond astonishing.

Then, in an unexpected development of his career, Hank got a call at his agency from someone he'd never heard of before.

"Hank, this is Jerry Perenchio at MCA concert booking."

"What can I do for you, sir?"

"I've been thinking this might be a good time to book you a tour. What do think?"

"That's awfully kind of you, Jerry. But, no thanks. I'm not a performer."

"Wait a minute, now. Hear me out."

"I'm sorry, Jerry. I'm just not interested. I've always disliked performing in public. Just ask my father. But thank you for thinking of me."

Jerry refused to give up. He continued to call until finally Hank decided to hear him out in person. Hank stopped by Jerry's office to hear his official pitch.

"Here's what I propose," Jerry said. "We're booking Johnny Mathis at the Seattle World's Fair. I thought it would be great to bill the Mancini Orchestra with Johnny for the weeklong engagement. You would do the first half of the show, Johnny would come out and do his half, and then you'd finish together with him singing 'Moon River.'"

Hank did find this idea intriguing, given that he wouldn't have to carry the entire show. He also thought it would be great to be part of the fair, also known as the Century 21 Exposition, that it was hoped would culturally revitalize the city through the arts, and new construction and structures, such as the now-famous Space Needle.

"Bring the family. You'll have a swell time!" Jerry said.

"I could do that?" Henry asked.

"Yes, absolutely."

"Okay, let me think it over."

Ginny loved the idea and thought it would be a wonderful opportunity. She told Hank that she, for one, would love the chance to hear his music performed live. The family accompanied him to Seattle for the week of shows booked at the Seattle Opera House. The first night, Hank was in a complete fog onstage. He froze and failed to say one word to the audience. But, somehow, he made it through the week and it was ultimately considered a very successful engagement. Despite how uncomfortable he'd been, he had to admit there was also something very gratifying about presenting his music to the public. He had only four hit songs at the time, so part of the challenge was designing the right pace and length of the show. He hadn't performed live since his days with Tex, Ginny, and the Glenn Miller Orchestra, back when he was a sideman and not in the spotlight. There would be a steep learning curve ahead of him if he wanted to continue doing live shows.

The press suddenly could not get enough of Hank, especially his hometown and company town newspaper, the *Los Angeles Times*. A reporter came to the house a few weeks before Christmas to interview the "Mancini Minstrels," which was what the family called themselves at Christmastime when they performed carols for friends and neighbors. Ginny brought the reporter a hot chocolate as Hank told him, "We're coming on stronger than ever this year. Chris here is adding trumpet to my piano on all our renditions of Christmas favorites."

"So, you're the leader, naturally?" the reporter asked.

"No, no. That would be Ginny. I can't sing."

"Everyone has their part to play," Ginny smiled.

"Yes, we do!" the twins said in unison.

"The one thing about Christmas, though . . ." Ginny began.

"Yes?" the reporter said, encouraging her to continue.

"Is that Hank comes up with more and more creative attempts to get out of decorating the tree," she laughed.

"She's right. I don't much like putting it up, but what I *really* don't like is taking it down," Hank confessed.

"None of us do!" Chris said.

"After a while, it becomes part of the family. It's like turning your back on an old friend who needs you," Hank said wistfully. "If it weren't about what the neighbors would think, we'd probably keep the tree up year-round."

Hank's Oscars and the success of *Breakfast at Tiffany's* made him a great asset at Paramount Pictures, which already had another assignment for him. They needed a composer to replace the score on the film *Hatari!*, directed by the legendary Howard Hawks and starring John Wayne. Leonard Maltin once called Hawks "the greatest American director who is not a household name." The original score had been done by Hoagy Carmichael, but the studio did not feel it suited the film. Hank was thrilled at the chance to work on an action film, which would give him the chance to stretch beyond sweet strings, flutes, and jazz. He was invited to meet with Hawks on the studio lot, and he was surprised to discover just how warm and affable Hawks was. As he walked into Hawks's office, the director greeted him by saying, "Do your worst, but no violins, no woodwinds, and none of that orchestral bunk!"

Hank laughed. "It's a pleasure to meet you, Mr. Hawks. And I agree."

"Please sit down. What can I get you?"

"Oh, nothing. I'm fine. Thank you."

"So, you're up for this African adventure?" Hawks asked.

"I really am," Hank said. "I've been thinking a lot about the instrumentation for this kind of score, and I feel strongly that it needs to reflect the geography of Africa and provide a backbone for the action sequences."

"I'm glad to hear you say that. In fact, I have my own collection of musical instruments I brought back from Africa. Would you like to see it?"

"Yes, I'd love to," Hank said excitedly. He was always looking to expand his sound palette in interesting new ways. Hawks brought out a huge box of authentic African instruments, and Hank first picked up a thumb piano and began to play around on the staggered tines that make up its different tones.

"They call that a mbira. Isn't it enchanting?"

"It really is."

Hank played a sweet improvised melody on the thumb piano.

"That's nice! I like that," Howard said.

Hank reached into the box and discovered more beautiful percussion instruments—gourds and giant pea pods, which were about two feet long.

"Those were dried in the sun. It's a wonderful sound they make."

"I'm sure I'll be able to put these to good use in the score. If I can borrow them, that is," Hank told him.

"Yes! I knew you were the right guy for this," Hawks said. Hank took this as an enormous compliment.

"Oh, and another thing," the director said.

"What's that, Mr. Hawks?"

"I also have some tape of the chants of the Maasai. Would you like to take them with you to listen to?"

"You'd better believe I would."

Listening to the recorded chants of the Maasai people gave

Hank a strong feel for the film. As he began to work up some musical ideas, he found out that Hawks had shot a lot of extra footage without any clear idea of how it might be used in the final film. Hank went to watch the footage with the editor and was struck by a particular sequence of the Italian actress Elsa Martinelli taking three baby pachyderms to a watering hole for a bath. Because elephants love to cool themselves with mud, Elsa would take them to the water, where they would fill up their trunks and spray themselves. She became the only person on the set who figured out how to feed the baby elephants, and they became very attached to her. When they began to follow her everywhere, it became obvious to Hawks that it had to be written into the film. The director came into the editing suite.

"Adorable, isn't it? Doesn't exactly advance the plot, though," he said.

Hank couldn't take his eyes off the screen, searching for ways to connect the images with the music.

"I'm probably going to have to cut that entire sequence. Unless you have any ideas?"

"I think I might," Hank said.

As Hank continued to watch the sequence, he noticed that the elephants were walking eight beats to the bar in a perfect boogie-woogie rhythm. It was all the inspiration he needed to write "Baby Elephant Walk." He imagined using a calliope as the main instrument on the song and found out there was only one electric calliope in the world—it was made by a man named Mr. Baccigalupi in Long Beach. Once Hawks heard Hank's "Baby Elephant Walk," he knew it had to stay, so he cut together a sequence in which John Wayne's character watches the playful scene of Martinelli and her elephant friends.

Hatari! contains another song by Hank and Johnny Mercer,

"Just for Tonight," but the breakout hit was the instrumental "Baby Elephant Walk," which surpassed the work of another veteran director yet again. When interviewed for the publicity of the film, Hank said, "I don't believe in this theory of film music not being noticed—it must be noticed in its place. In this elephant sequence, as in the opening of *Breakfast at Tiffany's*, if I hadn't made myself felt, I wouldn't have been serving the picture. You have to be felt at certain points. Where there is no dialogue, no sounds, just the visual—you'd better say something interesting. I don't know who started this theory of the best film music being that which you don't notice, but it isn't true." Hank's fans could not have agreed more—hearing overlooked and obscure instruments such as the accordion, French horn, or, in the case of *Hatari!*, a calliope, always felt exactly right and effortless in his scores.

After *Hatari!*, Hank went back to working with Blake Edwards, whose new film was *Days of Wine and Roses*, which starred Jack Lemmon in a surprising dramatic turn opposite actress Lee Remick. Edwards knew he wanted a title track song, as the title was taken from the lines of a Ernest Dowson poem: "They are not long, the days of wine and roses." Teaming up with Johnny Mercer once again, Hank played a melody he'd come up with over the phone for Johnny, who called back a few days later with a lyric.

Hank felt strongly that they had another winner and arranged for Blake and Jack Lemmon to hear it. The film was still in production and Hank found another empty space to debut it—this time a sound stage on the Warner Brothers lot.

They went in and Hank sat with his shoulder toward Blake and Jack while Johnny faced them. Hank began to play and John started singing what was probably the most personal and emotional lyric he'd ever written—about aging and the passage of time, two things he was grappling with then. Hank later recalled that upon finishing the song there was a "long, long, heavy, terrible silence." He thought it probably lasted ten seconds, but it seemed more like ten minutes. Finally, when he couldn't take it anymore, he swung around to look at them. Jack had a tear rolling down his cheek. Blake was choked up too. They both needed a few moments to take it in before saying anything.

The song is structurally unique, made up of only two sentences that match the song's two-part structure:

The days of wine and roses
laugh and run away
like a child at play
through a meadowland toward a closing door,
a door marked nevermore,
that wasn't there before
The lonely night discloses
just a passing breeze
filled with memories
of the golden smile that introduced me to
the days of wine and roses and you.

Its concentrated imagery and sophisticated harmonic language delivered the message powerfully, even without a bridge. The harmonies captured an underlying dread and foreshadowed the end of the happier days of the film's central couple due to alcoholism. Musically, Hank was inspired by the minor ninths he was brought up on when the big bands were being influenced by Ravel and Debussy, and when ballads took on the same lush modulations.

One morning over breakfast, Ginny came across a news item about the song.

"It says here that a promoter who was out working the *Days of Wine and Roses* record somewhere in the Midwest was involved in a head-on collision," she said.

Hank put down his coffee and the Blackwing pencil he was using to make some notations on a piece of music. "That's terrible. Is he okay?"

"Well, he is a she, who sustained a broken nose, fractured jaw bone, and a split upper lip, but is otherwise expected to make a full recovery." Ginny continued to read, "It says that at the time of impact she had a case of wine in the car—her gimmick for the promotion. When police arrived they thought she was slurring because of her busted lip, and then the policemen smelled the wine. She had a difficult time explaining that all she was guilty of was plugging Henry Mancini's latest song."

"Should we send wine? Or roses?" Hank asked. They started laughing as Monica walked into the kitchen.

"I'd say both," Ginny exclaimed.

"Sorry I had to leave the screening early for my rehearsal last night, Dad. How did it end, anyway?"

"With a French horn and a flat C," he smiled.

"Very funny, Dad. I meant the *movie*."

"Well, I suppose you're going to have to go see it," he said with a wink.

"Did you say you have another rehearsal tonight?" Ginny asked.

"Yup. I'll be home around eleven," Monica said.

Hank and Ginny were delighted to see Monica getting more and more serious about singing. She had a lovely voice.

When Oscar nomination time rolled around again, it was not nearly as surprising that Hank and Johnny were up for Best Song with "Days of Wine and Roses." For the second year in a row, Andy Williams was set to perform Hank's and Johnny's song at the Oscars. And, for the second year in a row, their song would win.

Hank joked with Andy after the show: "Hey, what if *you're* the good luck charm here? I'm going to have to insist you sing my song if I ever get nominated again!"

Andy smiled. "Nothing would make me happier, Hank."

"I hear they are working on booking some concert dates for us together," Hank said.

"Yes, now that you're getting used to hearing your own music in supermarkets or while you're on hold with the airlines, it's time to go out and share it with the world," Andy joked.

"Well, I can't think of a better chap to be on the road with," Hank said.

Andy released the album *Days of Wine and Roses and Other TV Requests* and it shot straight to the top of the charts and stayed there for sixteen weeks. Based on the tremendous sales of "Moon River," he was offered to host his own variety show on NBC. *The Andy Williams Show* ran from 1962 to 1971 and the Henry Mancini Orchestra was its first musical guest.

Now a three-time Oscar winner, Hank was fielding many offers. Producer Stanley Donen approached him to score *Charade*, another picture starring Audrey Hepburn and Cary Grant. This would be the first of fifteen films Hank would work on in London during the era of what some called "Hollywood-on-Thames," when American producers flooded London to take advantage of its exchange rate and lower labor costs.

Hank was set up with a rented piano in a penthouse suite in the Mayfair Hotel to work. There he crossed paths with a very talented American newcomer named Quincy Jones, who had just been hired for his first big movie score for *The Pawnbroker*. Quincy didn't know much about the particulars of film scoring and found a willing mentor in Hank, who became a close friend and source of support throughout Quincy's career.

Hank enjoyed exploring London and, after stumbling into an Indian gift shop once, found a treasure called a harmonium to add to his collection of exotic instruments. The reviews of *Charade* were superb—it was universally agreed that never before had the dual tones of humor and terror been so well captured.

While in London, Hank received an invitation that fully legitimized him in the minds of his children. The producers of an upcoming television special called *The Music of Lennon and McCartney*, which was shooting in Manchester, called and asked if Hank would perform a Beatles song of his choice on the show. Hank agreed and thoroughly enjoyed the day he spent hanging around John and Paul, who worked up a little bit for the show. Paul introduced Hank, who pretended not to know the two Beatles apart.

Paul introduced him this way: "One of the composers that John and I admire very much is Henry Mancini, known better to his friends as Hank. Ready, Henry?"

Then, as a joke, Hank, seated at the piano, replied, "Ready, *John*. I'm very happy that the boys asked me to come by to be on the show, and from their vast catalog I've picked one that I think is especially beautiful. It's called 'If I Fell.'"

Hank then proceeded to play the tune in a gorgeous arrangement of his own. The black and white filmography was lush, and the camerawork artful. The live audience was heard but not seen as the camera moved all over the minimally designed stage, with scaffolding surrounding an enormous concert grand piano. At the end of the song, John stepped in front of the camera and said, "Thank you, kind sir."

At the end of this particular stay in London, Hank phoned Blake Edwards.

"Blake! Just wanted to check in with you because I won't be easily reachable for the next week," he said.

"You're still in London?" Blake asked.

"Yes. Ginny is flying over to join me on the SS *France* back to New York for some downtime."

"The SS *France*, you say? Leaving what day?"

"Next Friday."

"Uncanny. I'm booked on the very same crossing."

Hank laughed gleefully. "Of course you are!"

"I'm going to be using the time to work on a new script called *The Pink Panther*."

"*Pink* panther?"

"It's a heist comedy. The pink panther is a priceless pink diamond. It has a flaw in the center that looks like a leaping panther."

"Sounds very intriguing."

"You're coming aboard, aren't you? And not just on the ocean liner—on the picture."

"You bet, Blake."

"We'll have plenty of time for me to fill you in more as we float merrily along."

There was much revelry on the high seas as they sailed headlong into their next great cinematic adventure, which would involve the creation of one most iconic characters and themes ever conceived.

Chapter Eleven

SCORING SUCCESS

What no one anticipated at the outset of making the 1963 film *The Pink Panther* was that it would have an animated opening credits sequence that would become an instant classic. The marriage of what was soon to be one of the most widely recognizable cartoon characters paired with one of the most memorable movie themes of all time amounted to a stroke of brilliance.

The theme from *The Pink Panther* is also one of the best examples of Hank's approach to writing with a specific musician in mind. In this case, it was the singular style of saxophonist Plas Johnson, a self-taught player from outside of New Orleans who grew up in a musical family. A multi-instrumentalist, Plas (his name is thought to have come from the French word *plaisant*, or pleasant) became most known for his tenor sax playing, but he also played alto and baritone sax, and some woodwind instruments, such as flutes and clarinet. He'd made a name for himself playing on the records of Peggy Lee, Nat King Cole, and Frank Sinatra, and became particularly known for his short, punchy solos. Hank noticed Plas's terrific style when he first started playing with the Mancini studio orchestra in the late 1950s, including on *Peter Gunn*. Over time, he'd grown to love the tone Plas coaxed out of his horn, which Hank referred to as "beefy." In describing his own playing, Plas thought of the notes he played as his words. "It's very boring if you keep using the same adjectives over and over again," Plas said. This is probably one reason many in the music world considered him the best improvisational tenor saxophonist of the time.

There was magic in the air on the day of the recording session for *The Pink Panther*. It is no exaggeration to say that everyone in the recording studio knew something extraordinary was happening. They were all impeccable professionals who could tell as soon as they laid their eyes on the score. Hank finished going over a few things with the engineers in the control room before entering the studio.

"Good afternoon, all," he said.

He picked up his baton as everyone settled back and made sure they had their sheet music in order. Then, as the red recording light went on, there was absolute silence. Hank's style of conducting was so understated that all it took were the slightest nods and gestures for him to communicate with his musicians. They played the piece down the first time and there was a feeling in the room that could only be described as both sobering and intoxicating; sobering because it carried with it the sound of Hollywood film history being made, and intoxicating to know that they were part of it.

"That sounded pretty good, everybody," Hank said. "Let's take it again."

After the second take, a mischievous grin crept across

Hank's face. Plas's solos exceeded Hank's expectations of just how full and fat the sound could be. The vibrations from Plas's horn could be felt on an almost cellular level. And then, to *everyone's* surprise, the string section stood up and applauded, which might have been the most astounding part of this historical day, since it is most unusual for the normally placid string section to stand up for anything.

Hank started to laugh. "I think that means we got it," he said. He could not have been more pleased, and went over to shake hands with Plas.

"You sure you don't want another take?" Plas asked.

"I've never been more sure of anything in my life. Thank you, Plas. That was exactly what I was hearing in my head. And so much more. Truly stellar, my friend."

"Thank you for writing it. It's awfully fun to play. How exactly did you ever come up with anything so perfect?"

"You know something?" Hank said. "I almost never start writing *before* I see a frame of film. But in this case, I couldn't stop thinking about all the tiptoeing around the phantom thief does. The more I thought about it, the 'dead-ant' progression just popped into my mind."

Plas laughed. "I like that. Dead-ant, dead-ant, dead-ant dead-ant dead-ant . . ." he sang to the tune of the song.

"It seemed to capture the essence of this debonair jewel thief. I wrote it thinking it would be for that character—until I got a load of that pink cat."

Plas and some of the other musicians chuckled.

"I knew it could work for both," Hank said.

"It really does," Plas agreed.

Some of the other players came around to thank Hank.

"So, wait. Someone just said that the guy who created Bugs

Bunny, Porky Pig, and Sylvester the Cat is the guy who drew the Pink Panther?" one of the session players asked.

"Yes, Friz Freleng, with his partner David DePatie," Hank said. "These animators are a funny bunch. They wanted the music to work to and I had to tell them, 'Sorry, guys, I'm used to working the other way around!' Leave it to Blake to even come up with the idea of an animation to open the film."

The Edwards and Mancini team was a winning one once again. For publicity on the film, Blake described having no qualms about giving Hank all the credit he deserved.

"There are times when I feel he's embellished the effectiveness of the scenes by fifty percent, he's made them come more alive than I had imagined. A lot of my success is due to his scoring," Blake said.

Likewise, Hank was more than happy to give his players their dues for bringing their own distinctive sounds to his recordings. Plas's unique way of articulating his notes blended with his deep level of soulfulness and amounted to musical alchemy. Hank made sure the musicians always knew how much they were appreciated by mentioning them by name in interviews so that other composers and producers would know about them and hire them too.

Blake needed another song for *The Pink Panther* for the actress Fran Jeffries to sing on camera in a performance set piece. Set primarily in Italy, a ski lodge in Cortina d'Ampezzo in the Italian Alps is where the characters gathered in the evenings. Blake wanted the song to have a jet-set feel to it and to be sung in Italian. Given that Blake had gone into production almost immediately after finishing the script, things were moving quickly. He summoned Hank to Rome to work on this song. On the flight, Hank wrote a wonderfully fun, swanky tune on the back of a menu. He knew he was going to need an Italian lyricist for the words and thought of Franco Migliacci, who'd written the lyrics for an enormous hit called "Volare." Once Hank got to Italy, he got together with Franco, who wrote the words and the song became "Meglio Stasera." Hank once again called upon Johnny Mercer, who wrote the English words that made the song known as "It Had Better Be Tonight." The song is performed in the film during a sassy and humorous scene in which Jeffries sings and dances while she roves through the crowd in the ski lodge's lobby and makes Inspector Clouseau dance with her.

During production in Rome, Hank brought Ginny over to join him. He thought it would be a good time to make a roots trip to the town where his father was born. Not wanting to brave the roads as they were then, Hank hired a car to take them to the hilly town of Scanno in the Abruzzi region. It was a formidable landscape filled with jagged rocks and hills, and almost no tree cover. Hank stared out the window pensively.

"Quinto *walked* from here to Naples?" Ginny asked him.

"It was a route without roads back then."

It was almost impossible for Hank to imagine making a trip like that.

"This car ride is four hours, so how long would that have taken him on foot?" Ginny asked.

"Weeks. All to board that ship in Naples and sail to America."

The car began to climb the hill upon which the town of Scanno was spread out. It was a charming, classic Italian village with cobblestone streets and pale stone houses marked with soot from the kitchen fires. Known for being difficult to reach,

Scanno did not get many tourists in those days. One of the remarkable things about it is the traditional garb of its women, who only wore black.

"You see the women. They still dress in the old way," the driver told them.

"And they carry things on their heads? I don't think I've never seen that in Italy before," Hank replied.

"Yes. There are some scholars who believe that the Scannesi people actually come from the Orient."

Ginny thought she might have misheard. "Did you say the *Orient*?"

"You know, the scholars, they argue," the driver said. "But Scanno is called 'a place of Oriental flavor.' The dialect, the women's dress, and the traditions and customs may have survived because of their geographic and cultural isolation."

"Fascinating," Ginny said.

"Oh, and the lace made here," the driver told them, "is some of the most beautiful and intricate of any in the world."

Laundry was strung up across most of the archways in the village. Hank and Ginny got out of the car to go inside the church of Santa Maria di Costantinopoli and see the beautiful fresco of the Madonna in throne. Then they returned to the car. Hank saw no reason to spend much more time there.

"It's not really an overnight kind of town," he told Ginny.

"We can find another town nearby to stay if you'd like to spend a little more time," she said.

He opened the car door for her and said, "No, that's all right." Hank climbed back into the car. "We're ready to go back to Rome," he told the driver.

"Yes, of course, Mr. Mancini," he said. One of the big perks to being in Italy was that everyone knew how to properly pronounce Mancini—with the *ch* sound, not Man-*see*-nee.

"But first you must see the heart-shaped lake," the driver told them and took a different road out of town so they could stand on the hillside to see the shape of it from above. Sure enough, it was formed into a perfect heart.

"Hank, he wasn't kidding. It's a heart," Ginny said.

"Dad always did have a funny way of showing his love," Hank said.

When they returned to Rome, Hank had to jump back into work. As much as he was enjoying himself on the picture, it was not without conflict—especially whenever he found himself mediating between Blake and star Peter Sellers, who had not been Blake's first choice for the role of Inspector Clouseau. It had been a blow for Blake to lose Peter Ustinov, who was originally cast but backed out. With pre-production in full swing, Blake had to act quickly and came up with the idea of Peter Sellers, who was relatively unknown then. Much to his relief, Sellers came aboard within days, saving the production great cost. Inspector Clouseau was not the lead role in the script, but it didn't take long for Peter Sellers to literally begin stealing the show. *The Pink Panther* became one of the highest-grossing comedy franchises of the time and it seemed there was no one who hadn't seen it. There was no doubt about this when they received the following invitation:

His Royal Highness the Prince Charles
requests your presence
at a showing of
The Pink Panther.

One film a year was chosen as part of the United Kingdom's Cinema and Television Benevolent Fund to raise money for charity and Hank was honored to be part of the tradition. But in a case of royal oversight, Sellers's invitation was addressed only to him and did not include his current lady friend. He was so upset he couldn't bring her that he refused to attend the command performance. When Hank and Ginny met Prince Charles, he was quite humorous regarding the snafu with Sellers. In a silly voice he told them, "The next time, I shall *command* him to be here." Everyone involved with the making of *The Pink Panther* assumed it would be one and done, but the movie was such a smash hit that Blake knew there would need to be a sequel. Peter Sellers was already contracted to do a film adaptation of a Broadway play *A Shot in the Dark* but was unhappy with the script. He asked Blake to consider rewriting it and Blake could see right away how it could be adapted for Inspector Clouseau, so it was quite by accident that it became the next film in the *The Pink Panther* series. The harmonium Hank had picked up in London and had been waiting to use became the inspiration for the score for *A Shot in the Dark*, which was released just months after *The Pink Panther*.

Hank continued to pursue touring in addition to the scoring work he was doing during this period. He was growing more and more confident as a live conductor and began to enjoy it once he really figured out how to make it work. It didn't take him long to realize that trying to rehearse a new band in every city was going to burn him out quickly. So, he turned to Freddie Dale, who'd become Hank's right-hand man in the booking company Jerry Perenchio formed after leaving MCA. Freddie was a short, funny, chain-smoking Italian who became one of Hank's greatest friends. It was Freddie who came up with the idea to hire his pal Al Cobine from the University of Indiana to contract the twenty string players that made up half of the forty-piece orchestra at that time.

At one engagement at the Greek Theatre, Hank's hometown gig in Los Angeles, the show went over so well that the audience treated Hank and his orchestra to an unexpected standing ovation. Afterwards, Quinto pulled Hank aside.

"I think you need to take some conducting lessons," he told him.

By now, Hank was well practiced in the art of not taking anything his father said too personally. After all, 1963 was also the year *Billboard* magazine published its list of half-million sellers—LPs that sold a half million or more. Included on the list was both *The Music from Peter Gunn* and *Breakfast at Tiffany's*.

On June 26, 1963, Hank experienced what he later called "one of the most moving moments" of his life when he and Ginny tuned into the television to watch President John F. Kennedy's arrival in Berlin, Germany. Just before Kennedy began what is considered to be one of his best speeches—the "Ich bin ein Berliner (I am a Berliner)" speech—they played "Moon River." Hank found out from Andy that it was one of the president's favorites and he specifically requested it for the occasion.

Hank and Andy Williams had begun touring a lot together. Just five months after Kennedy's speech, they were headed to the South to start a few weeks of tour dates before the holidays. Freddie Dale traveled as a road manager with Hank on most of these trips. When Hank and Freddie arrived in Tulsa, there was an urgent message at the hotel from Ginny. Freddie accompanied Hank to his room, where he called home immediately.

"Sweetheart, I'm very sorry," Ginny said. "Your father has passed away. He had a heart attack."

Hank fell silent.

"I'll take care of all the arrangements. Quinto mentioned a while ago that he wanted a solemn requiem mass. Is that all right with you?" Ginny asked.

"Yes. Of course," Hank said.

"I love you, darling."

"Love you too."

Hank felt numb. He hung up the phone and turned to Freddie. "My father has passed."

"I'm very sorry, Hank. Shall I cancel the show?"

"No, let's do it."

After their few dates in the South, Hank flew home to bury his father. He took solace in the idea of him being reunited with his mother where they could rest in peace together.

A couple weeks later, Hank and Andy began another string of dates with the Osmonds before the holidays. When they landed at Midway Airport in Chicago on November 22, they got off the plane to find the terminal eerily silent.

"What in the world is going on?" Hank asked Andy.

"I don't know, but something bad has happened," Andy answered. "Listen."

Hank's furrowed brow expressed his disorientation. As he looked around the room, the only sound that could be heard was crying. Everywhere, people were hugging one another and crowding around the televisions.

Hank and Andy cautiously approached one of the screens and realized that the president had been shot. They stood thunderstruck and suddenly became as paralyzed as everyone else in the terminal.

The world had changed in an instant.

They finally found their way to a cab and sat mostly in silence as the images from the television played over and over in their minds—the convertible black presidential limousine, the waving of the president and the first lady to the people of Dallas who lined the streets, and the spray of blood.

When they arrived at their hotel, Hank called home. "Hi, Gin," he said.

She sighed audibly. "Are you in Chicago?"

"Yes. We arrived safely."

She started to cry. "I just can't stop thinking about seeing the president lay that wreath at the Tomb of the Unknown Soldier on Veteran's Day. It was only two days after your father passed . . . And, I don't know, the image brought me comfort, for some reason. And now he's gone too."

"I know. I just . . ."

Ginny interjected, "And you know Jackie rarely travels with him on political trips. Why on earth did she have to be there for this?"

"Andy and I left a message for Bobby. We're trying to figure out whether or not to do the show tomorrow. Tonight has been cancelled, of course."

The Bobby whom Hank was referring to was Bobby Kennedy. Andy and his wife, Claudine, were friendly with the Kennedys after they'd met skiing in Sun Valley. None of what was happening felt real. The promoter in Chicago called to tell them they needed to make a decision about the show the following night as soon as they could. The next morning, Hank awoke only to relive the nightmare all over again. Glued to the television, Hank and Andy finally decided that the show must go on as their small way of trying to provide some solace to people—or a distraction, at the very least. That night, there was not an empty seat in the show at the five-thousand capacity Arie Crown Theater in Chicago.

Hank began the show without a mention of the tragedy. He'd begun to develop a strong sense of his audience, and could tell instinctively when some comic relief was appropriate. About halfway through the show, the forty-piece orchestra went into David Rose's "The Stripper," which received instant applause and did in fact provide some slight relief from the heaviness that hung in the air. The levity led the way for Hank to take a seat at the piano.

"This section of the show is to justify fifteen years of piano lessons," he told the grieving audience.

He began with "Days of Wine and Roses," then led into a medley of other Academy Award winners. This was followed by a serendipitous part of the show when the youngest and fifth Osmond brother, Donny, came out to make his debut performance. The five-year-old brought the house down with his solo rendition of "You Are My Sunshine." After that, it was abundantly clear they'd made the right choice to go on with the show and cap it with a great hope for the next generation.

"Now we're going to do something that is a little out of my current style, but perhaps tonight has a very special meaning," Hank said, and they finished the night with "Stars and Stripes Forever."

Andy told the crowd, "I must say, we had a little problem deciding whether to perform or not. If we've succeeded in giving you a couple hours of pleasure in this otherwise terrible week, it was all worthwhile."

~

Later in the year, when the reviews for *Charade*, starring Audrey Hepburn, came out, Hank had reason to celebrate. He'd taken some great risks with that score that had begun to pay off. The film's mix of humor and suspense was not an easy mood to capture, but somehow he'd figured out how to strike just the right balance.

One morning, the twins walked into the kitchen with the latest issue of *Billboard* magazine.

"Read it, read it!" Felice yelled at Monica, who was waving it around. Then Felice grabbed it and cleared her throat, which made her sister giggle. She performed it like a soliloquy.

"'The score is imaginative, fresh, hauntingly melodic, and does much to build the mood of the flick,'" she read. "'Main emphasis, however, is bound to be on the strange combination of chilling mystery and comic suspense that *Charade* seems to convey . . . So tastefully is everything blended together, that one gets to the end of the picture scared stiff, but chuckling out of the corner of his mouth.'"

Monica started clapping. "Bravo, Daddy!" she said.

Ginny had to laugh.

By 1964, the Mancini kids were outgrowing their Northridge house and Hank was looking to move closer to town to shorten his commute. He and Ginny were both taken aback when some of their neighbors came to their door after the For Sale sign went up in the front yard.

"We hope when you begin considering offers that you're sensitive to the makeup of the families on the block. We'd all like to continue to keep that consistent," one of them said.

"I'm not sure I understand," Hank told them, even though he did.

"We know you'll do the right thing."

Hank shut the door and turned to Ginny. He was fuming. "What gives people the idea that they are superior over other human beings?" he asked her.

"They probably wouldn't like it if they knew I was half Mexican either," Ginny said.

"I absolutely loathe bigots," he told her.

"I know, sweetheart. Me too."

Hank found it preposterous and offensive that these neighbors, whom they'd known for many years now, would have the nerve to say such a thing. He was always shocked at these moments when he realized how much prejudice and racism continued to permeate society and culture because, from where he stood, he thought things were improving. With musicians, there was always the greatest mix of people who came from everywhere and from every background. That was the beauty of it.

Just as they were dealing with this issue in their personal lives with the selling of their house, Hank received a troubling phone call from a film executive at Universal that further made this point.

"Hank, it's Harry from Universal. Do you have a minute?"

"Sure. What can I do for you?"

"We've got a picture over here—*Mirage*, starring Gregory Peck and Walter Matthau."

"Sounds like a great cast."

"Don't worry, I'm not trying to recruit you. But I am calling to get your opinion on someone."

"Who's that?"

"His name's Quincy Jones?"

"Quincy's excellent."

"But . . ."

"Incredibly talented," Hank told him.

"But, you see—"

"No, I'm afraid I don't."

"Well, how can I put this delicately?"

"You probably can't. Look, you called for my opinion and I'm giving it to you."

"Sure, but it would only be his second feature film."

"Have you seen *The Pawnbroker*? Snatch him up while you still can. I have a feeling he is going to do *very* well."

"It's just . . . Well, do you really think a black man could handle a dramatic picture?"

Hank was really beginning to lose his patience. "He's excellent. You couldn't do any better. I have to go now, Harry."

And Hank hung up the phone.

The new house was a white brick Georgian mansion in Holmby Hills, a pocket between Bel Air and Beverly Hills. It had once been owned by radio and television star Art Linkletter and was still on some of the maps to stars' homes, so once in a while an awkward stranger would come to the door and ask if Mr. Linkletter was home. Humphrey Bogart and Lauren Bacall, Judy Garland, Bing Crosby, and Sammy Cahn had also all lived on that street at one point. The new place was a major lifestyle change for the kids, who no longer had the benefit of being able to ride up and down the block on bikes with their friends, drop the bikes on the front lawn, and run in and out of the house all afternoon with the screen door slamming behind them.

This was a stately home on a quiet street where everything happened behind formidable gates and privacy walls. The twins were fiercely competitive and needed some independence from each other going into their teen years. While shopping for their new home, Hank and Ginny were specifically looking for a house that had two *identical*-sized rooms. The day they closed escrow, they drove the girls to see the new house, and it was as if they didn't care about anything else but that. They ran straight upstairs to measure off the bedrooms foot by foot to ensure the rooms, like them, were indeed identical. The new house had more space for Hank to paint, a hobby he'd picked up over time. It had started with charcoals and drawing, and then he moved to pen and ink, markers, and finally, watercolors.

"It clears my mind," he told Ginny.

When asked by a *Los Angeles Times* reporter who came to profile the family in their new home if he was taking any instruction, Hank joked, "No. I don't want to spoil a good thing."

In 1965, Andy Williams and his wife, Claudine, invited the Mancinis to join them for the holidays to ski in Sun Valley, Idaho. Up to that point, Hank and Ginny had been spending Christmas in Hawaii, because it was a good time to have the kids out of school for vacation. They were thrilled at the invitation to join Andy, Claudine, and their children for a snowy holiday. The Williamses had become even closer friends with Bobby and Ethel Kennedy and their kids, who spent holidays there, and the Mancinis were immediately welcomed into the fold. Spending the holiday in Sun Valley soon became their new family tradition. There, Hank first learned to ski and immediately fell in love with it—nothing else brought him such peace as zipping down a mountain while breathing in all that fresh air, even if it was a bit thinner. One year, Jackie Kennedy invited the entire Mancini family over to watch her home movies. Hank and Ginny were surprised and delighted to find that she'd used the theme from *Peter Gunn* to underscore all of John's scenes.

Hank and Ginny had built an amazing life for themselves. They were on solid footing financially and Ginny, as much as she loved working, thought it best to stop and leave the work for singers who needed to make a living. She felt such a strong calling to help singers who'd fallen on hard times and began to spend more time working to help them. She and Hank were becoming dedicated philanthropists, as Hank also endowed scholarships at several university music programs. The two felt extremely blessed to be surrounded with such lovely friends and did their best to help facilitate connections for others. In 1966, Quincy and his expectant wife, Ulla, moved from London to Los Angeles.

"Hank, wouldn't it be nice if we threw them a baby shower to introduce them to some new friends?" Ginny asked one day.

"That's a wonderful idea, Gin. I can invite the Newmans as a surprise for Quincy. He absolutely idolizes Alfred."

Hank was referring to film composer Alfred Newman, who'd scored *All About Eve*, *How the West Was Won*, *The Diary of Anne Frank*, and dozens of other films.

"Oh, he will be thrilled to meet Alfred!" Ginny said.

The shower was a who's who of people in the film and music business. Quincy was stunned when he saw Alfred Newman walk in and was extremely grateful to Hank and Ginny for arranging the party. Quincy hit it off instantly with Alfred, who began inviting him to his famous five-thirty post-time cocktail parties in his Frank Lloyd Wright–designed estate on Sunset Boulevard. This is where the Newman sons allegedly bowled using their father's eight Oscars as pins. Alfred became another mentor to Quincy, and their personal and professional relationship proved invaluable as Quincy made his way into the business as a formidable newcomer. It made a big difference in those early years of his career to have the benefit of such incredible guidance of veterans like Hank and Alfred. When Quincy was hired to write the music for the television series *Ironside* for a forty-four-piece orchestra, Hank would often drop by his sessions to see how things were going and to look over Quincy's scores. On one of Hank's visits early on in the first season, he was dumbfounded to see the complexity of what Quincy was writing.

"Q, this is like a damn symphony. Look at all these sixteenth and thirty-second notes. How much music are you doing for this episode?"

Quincy looked down at his notes. "Forty-four minutes."

Hank's eyes went wide. "*Forty-four*? Is that typical for this show?"

"Seems like it."

"You're writing forty-four minutes of music weekly like it's a feature film. This is TV, Q—use whole notes, long-sustained passages with your strings and your horns. Let a solo instrument, your rhythm section, or your bass player do the dancing on top. Don't try to write Stravinsky's *The Firebird* suite for every episode, or you'll never live through the year."

Q laughed and took the advice to heart.

In 1966, Hank teamed up with Blake again for the comedy *What Did You Do in the War, Daddy?*, featuring Carroll O'Connor. Hank was proud of this picture and was disappointed it did not achieve the level of success it should have. He followed that project with a Stanley Donen film, *Arabesque*, starring Sophia Loren and Gregory Peck. As *Charade* and *Arabesque* were both Donen films, Hank was about to hit the Donen trifecta when he received a phone call from one of his favorite people regarding the next project on the director's slate. It was Audrey Hepburn, calling from the south of France.

"Hank," she said. He heard her voice in the unmistakable way she had of singing his name. "I've just signed on to a new picture with Stanley called *Two for the Road.* It's with me and the wonderful Albert Finney. Dearest Hank, please, won't you do the music? I can't imagine anyone else but you scoring. I told Stanley I would call you myself to ask."

This was the only time the star of a picture ever called to ask Hank to do the music. With Audrey Hepburn on the other end of the line, how could he say no? The nonlinear structure of *Two for the Road* made it ahead of its time and, despite being a critical success with outstanding performances and music, it was not a box-office hit. The music was classic Mancini, featuring the specific sound of solo musicians. This time, it was the grandfather of jazz violinists, Stéphane Grappelli, who cofounded the Quintette du Hot Club de France with guitarist Django Reinhardt. This was one of the many films Hank worked on in London and he was thrilled to find out that Grappelli was available to record and currently in Paris. They brought him to London, and when he entered the studio, the entire string section began tapping their bows on their instruments—their accolade for a great artist. It was one of those days that Hank had to pinch himself at this life of his that allowed him to meet and work with the world's greatest musicians.

Later that year, Hank went to work on another Audrey Hepburn film, a thriller called *Wait Until Dark*, directed by Terence Young. It was a chilling tale in which Audrey's character was a blind woman terrorized by a group of criminals, who were convinced their stolen goods were inside a doll in her apartment.

This story offered Hank a chance to get very creative in

order to support the dark mood and narrative. He came up with the idea of intentionally detuning a second piano to double the first piano for an extremely unsettling effect. When reports came out that the film's audiences were literally feeling sick, he knew he'd achieved this goal.

When he received a phone call from his old friend Jack one day, Hank figured this was what he was calling to talk about. Jack was still a high school marching bandleader in Cleveland, where his students were winning lots of honors. Jack was a talented and exacting musician and he seemed to be enjoying the work.

"Hank, there's something I'd like to ask you about," Jack said. "Now, I know the chances are very slim with your schedule these days, but I promised the students I would ask."

"What is it, Jack?" Henry asked.

"Would you consider being the guest conductor for the school's spring concert fundraiser?"

"That sounds like a lot of fun, Jack. When is it?"

"April 16."

"Well, that's my birthday!"

"Oh, how could I forget? Listen, I'll understand if you can't get away then—"

"Nonsense, it would be my absolute pleasure. It'll be extra festive!"

The event was a tremendous success, with Hank conducting the award-winning high school band playing "The Pink Panther," "Peter Gunn," and "Moon River." Toward the end of the show, there was some commotion in the audience as Hank returned to the stage, piccolo in hand. Jack always ended his concerts with "Stars and Stripes Forever" so a student could play the piccolo part, and now Hank was doubling that very lucky student. The audience cheered wildly. They all felt incredibly honored to have Henry Mancini participate in their event and make it so unforgettable. Backstage after the show, Jack brought out a birthday cake in the shape of a piano for Hank. Everyone sang to him and a student cut the cake. Someone handed Hank the first piece, but he insisted that Jack have it for doing such a fine job with the band, who clearly had worked hard under his leadership.

"Henry, I can't tell you how grateful I am that you would do this for us," Jack said.

"I'm more than happy to. You know that. Plus, I get the added bonus of spending my birthday with my oldest friend."

Jack fell quiet for a moment and Hank sensed a shift in Jack's mood. He began to brace himself for some kind of bad news.

"Jack, is everything all right?"

"Yes. Forgive me. I wanted to tell you a story about your father. I meant to tell you shortly after he passed and never got around to it."

"My father?"

"It's from a very long time ago, but I always thought you should know."

"What is it?" Henry asked.

"It may seem silly now, but I know how hard he always was on you, even after you'd reached a level of success most people never attain."

Hank sat quietly, his signal for Jack to keep talking.

"You remember how, after graduation, I stayed in West Aliquippa and kept working at the plant the first year after high school to save up for college?" Jack said.

"Sure."

"Well, your father was a supervisor at that point and he oversaw an assembly line. Don't you know he would literally stop production on the line, making the men wait while he caught me up on all of your news and accomplishments? He was so proud of you, Hank. And I know he never told you himself because he just didn't know how."

Hank had never heard anything like this about his father before and it touched him very deeply after all those years.

Hank continued to tour with Andy in Japan and they later did three sold-out shows at the Royal Albert Hall in London. Hank and Ginny took all three kids to Japan and other international destinations where he was performing—Israel, all over Europe, and a boat trip through Italian islands.

Andy and Hank became involved with Bobby Kennedy's presidential campaign after he announced his run as the Democratic candidate on March 16, 1968. On May 24, they took part in a benefit concert for the campaign at the Los Angeles Memorial Sports Arena—along with Jerry Lewis, Gene Kelly, and Sonny and Cher—that was put on by the S.R.O. All Stars—Standing Room Only for Robert F. Kennedy. Hank found Bobby's speech that night incredibly inspiring and it reinforced his feeling that Bobby was the candidate who could unite the country.

Bobby won the primary after a grueling campaign that had him constantly running back and forth between northern and southern California. While Hank was in his dressing room before a performance at the Sahara Casino in Lake Tahoe, a news alert came on the television that said Bobby Kennedy had been shot. It happened just minutes after his victory speech at the Ambassador Hotel in Los Angeles. Hank was frozen in shock, but he knew he had a show to do and that no one out there had this news yet. He thought maybe Bobby could pull through and prayed for this all throughout his performance. When he found out that Bobby died, he felt sick. It was another terrible American tragedy he felt very close to and wished he had more answers for.

With President Richard Nixon in the White House the following year, Hank and Ginny found that not everyone in their social circle was pleased with them for accepting an invitation to an official dinner.

"The White House belongs to every American," Ginny told him.

"You are absolutely right," Hank agreed.

In fact, they were honored to be included in such an intimate dinner for the Apollo 11 astronauts and their wives. Hank was asked to play a piano that was in terrible shape and barely in tune. He was astounded by how bad it was. Afterwards, the president asked Hank to accompany him upstairs.

"Can I show you my record collection?" Nixon asked.

"Of course, Mr. President."

The president walked over to the cabinet that held his albums and pulled one out.

"This here is my favorite," he said. It was "Victory at Sea," the theme from the documentary television series of the same name about naval warfare during World War II. The music is sweeping and epic, a celebration of what many Americans call the greatest generation.

"Ah, Richard Rodgers. Wonderful composer. The only

person to win the EGOT," Hank commented. He could see the president was puzzled and explained further, "It's an acronym for Emmy, Grammy, Oscar, and Tony awards."

"And you haven't won the EGOT yet?"

"No, I only have the EGO."

Both of them laughed, then Nixon handed Hank a few of his other favorites.

"I play these for hours," Nixon said. It was a small pile of Lawrence Welk records. Hank looked them over. "And, of course, Pat and I love 'Moon River.'"

"Thank you, Mr. President. That's very kind."

Like others who visited at the Nixon White House, Hank and Ginny couldn't help notice the roaring fireplace in the middle of June, while the air conditioning was churning away. The Nixons found the Mancinis gracious guests and invited them back for an official state dinner with Italian Prime Minister Emilio Colombo, which almost every prominent Italian in America attended.

Later that summer, there was an unexpected twist in Hank's career. He'd recorded a song that had been written by the Italian film composer Nino Rota called "Love Theme from *Romeo and Juliet*" for Franco Zeffirelli's 1968 film, *Romeo and Juliet.* One night in Orlando, a radio DJ at WLOF, a rock station, gave it a spin very late—maybe after he thought the kids had all gone to bed. But as soon as the song finished, the phone lines began lighting up like fireworks. People were going crazy for it. Even Hank couldn't explain it, as the timing was right smack at the height of the rock and roll. This was precisely why some stations resisted playing it, finding it too middle of the road for their programming. MOR was an actual genre then, and not one that most teens or twenty-somethings wanted to be associated with—or so the conventional wisdom went. After the song hit number one, all the stations were forced to play it in order to appease their listeners who demanded it.

Hank was painting at home one day when he got a call from the record company. "We thought you might like to know that you just kicked the Beatles' 'Get Back' out of first place," they told him.

"Well, that should make my teenagers either very proud or completely mortified," he said dryly.

This was a feat Hank had not even accomplished with his other colossal hits, "Peter Gunn," "Moon River," or "The Pink Panther." Most fans of the "Love Theme" didn't even realize the piece was composed by Rota—they just assumed it was a Mancini original. It went on to win a Grammy for Best Instrumental Arrangement. And just like the waltz "Moon River," no one could ever seem to explain why this anti-rock establishment record touched the younger generation of listeners as deeply as it did.

Chapter Twelve

THE MANCINI GENERATION

At the apex of their teen years, the twins were like almost every other American teenager of their generation—enamored with Elvis. Hank had his own curiosity about the gyrating rock star, despite being outside of the rock and roll world, strictly speaking. Ginny, who was always up for an adventure, especially when it coincided with family time, suggested to Hank that they take the girls to Las Vegas to see Elvis in concert. As they arrived at the entrance of the venue at the Sahara Hotel and Casino, Hank was instantly pulled aside by a female journalist who was surely closer to his age than to Elvis's. The twins shot each other a look—both were mixed with equal amounts of annoyance and pride to see their dad stealing some of the pre-show spotlight.

"Henry Mancini. One of the *top* names in the world of music," the journalist said, her coiffed hair bouncing as she threw her head back. "You must be so very busy. You're always busy!"

"Yes. I'm working on a picture with Blake Edwards directing.

It's called *Darling Lili* with the incomparable Julie Andrews and Rock Hudson. But I've been very much looking forward to tonight's event and happy to be here with my wife, Ginny, and our two daughters."

"Are you an Elvis fan too?"

"Mr. Presley is an institution. He has longevity. People keep saying, 'What's a rock star going to do once he hits thirty?' Well, we're going to see what he does!"

Hank was completely confident handing out compliments to rock stars, having once knocked the Beatles out of the number-one spot himself.

It's not that Hank had any kind of strong *dislike* of rock music. He was always striving to stay current and to challenge himself. One of his most impressive forays into rock and roll was in 1970, when he conducted the rock opera *Tommy*, written by the Who's Pete Townshend at the Hollywood Bowl. The *Los Angeles Times Music Review* wrote, "Only Mancini could make such mass-scale orchestral sense out of all those rock guitar chords."

Hank augmented the orchestra with a chorus of eight men and eight women, reserving two of the spots for Monica and Felice. Both twins and Chris had been singing on Hank's RCA records since they were in their early teens, and it was always a meaningful experience for them to see their father outside of the parent role and in the professional world, where he was so beloved. They developed a mature respect for his immense gifts and his gracious style of dealing with people. The first year the twins went away to college, Felice wrote a poem as a Christmas gift to her parents. Leaving home made her realize just how much they had done for her and how well loved she was:

Sometimes
Not often enough
We reflect upon
The good things
And those thoughts
Usually center
Around those
We love
And I think about
Two people
Who mean so much
To me
And for so many years
Have made me so
Very happy
And I count
The times
I have forgotten
To say
Thank you
And just how much
I love them

Hank read the poem aloud to Ginny. He was especially touched by it, being someone who was not always able to express his love for others through spoken words, preferring to let his art do the talking.

"This is so beautiful," he said.

"Bless her heart," Ginny added.

"Just when you think they can't stand you," he laughed.

"You know better than that."

"I think this could be a song."

"Then I'd say it's in good hands," she teased.

"What do you think of the title 'Sometimes'?"

"Perfect," she said.

Hank took the poem to the piano and within a couple of hours had written something breathtaking. He was trying to think of an artist for whom the song would be a good fit when he remembered that the Carpenters were looking for material for a new album. He called his friend Sally Stevens, one of the top film singers and vocal contractors, to cut a demo of the song with her. In the next few days, the demo was sent to Richard and Karen Carpenter, who fell instantly in love with it and wanted to record it. It went on the album *Carpenters*, which sold well beyond platinum status. It is the only song that Felice would ever write, as she chose not to pursue music professionally. Monica, on the other hand, later became a Grammy nominated vocalist.

As his eleventh film with Blake, *Darling Lili* was quickly becoming a different kind of animal. For the first time, Hank was privy to much of the behind-the-scenes drama he was usually insulated from. Blake had been somewhat at odds with the studio at the outset of the production, and by the end of it he was ready to leave the business altogether. Hank felt terrible about the challenges Blake was up against. To begin with, the studio insisted that Blake shoot the picture in Europe, despite his being vehemently against it. Then there was the complication of Blake being in a romantic relationship with his star, Julie Andrews, and being forced to navigate the particular challenges that came with mixing his work and personal lives. Some even saw *Darling Lili* as an elaborate wedding gift from Blake to Julie once they decided they would marry. When Blake and Julie first got together, Hank and Ginny were baffled, as were most of Blake's other friends. Blake was thirteen years her senior and they seemed a total mismatch in almost every other way as well.

"How did you two first meet?" Hank remembered asking him.

"It's actually kind of a funny story," Blake told him.

"That's not surprising."

Blake smiled at Hank's dryly humorous tone. "I was on the way in to see my analyst and she was on her way out!" he said.

Hank wasn't sure meeting someone while crossing paths at the psychiatrist's office heralded a strong future for a relationship, but who was he to say?

"Pretty corny, right?"

"Noooooo," Hank said, wanting to show his friend support.

"Anyway, that was years ago," Blake said. "But we'd started seeing each other recently. And she told me, by the way, how much the sessions with the doc were helping her, so it restored my faith in it. We made a deal that we are just going to take our relationship one day at a time."

Blake and Julie married in November of 1969 during the production of *Darling Lili* and remained married for forty-one years, until his death. As time went on, Hank and Ginny and their friends got to know Julie better, and they understood the relationship more. They grew to adore her and see that she and Blake made a wonderful, if not unconventional, couple. Julie, of course, had many dimensions not known to the public—many of whom actually believed that she *was* Mary Poppins, despite that being a fictional character.

In *Darling Lili*, a musical set during World War I, Julie

played opposite Rock Hudson as a femme fatale and spy whose cover is that of a popular British music hall performer. The film's production began in late 1967 and ran into major weather problems in Europe, as well as student-led political protests against capitalism in France the following year that interfered with shooting. When the budget inevitably began spiraling out of control, the studio blamed Blake.

Hank was working on his end of things in Los Angeles, and even though it was normal in their process for Blake not to hear any of the music until it was time to record it, *Darling Lili* was different because it was a musical. Like a stage musical, the songs are an integral part of the storytelling and need to propel the narrative, making the process much more complex. Hank couldn't remember another time when he got so many visits from studio executives. They began to casually pop in on him to ask his opinion on various songs—what should stay and what should go, and what scene a certain song would work best in.

What he didn't realize was that no matter how he answered their questions, they were twisting his words when they would later speak to Blake, attempting to strong-arm him into doing things their way based on Hank's alleged support. The manipulation worked to distance the director from his own project and dragged Hank right in the middle of studio politics.

He didn't understand the extent of the damage until it had already been done and had nearly destroyed his long and deep relationship with Blake. It reached the point where they weren't speaking much at all, and by the time production wrapped it was clear the studio was going to take the film away from Blake for the final cut. Blake and Julie were so soured from the experience that they wanted to get as far away from Hollywood as possible. They moved to Switzerland in an effort to renew their spirits and reassess their lives. Without the benefit of his and Blake's partnership, Hank was going to have to navigate a new decade without the rudder that had been steering his boat for so long.

As it turned out, Hank did not have to wonder long about his next project. In 1970, Paramount Pictures hired him for another film that needed its original score replaced: *The Molly Maguires*, based on the 1876 Irish coal miners' strike in Pennsylvania. Hank saw the project as a rare opportunity to show his dramatic side, having recently come to the realization that he was fighting against his own success much of the time for being known as a composer of mostly lighter fare. He relished the chance to tackle a more ethnic model that this score would require in both instrumentation and harmonics. The main theme he created for the film featured accordion and evoked a nostalgic melancholy—something he was ready to express after the events of the 1960s. He certainly had the depth and the talent for creating an intensely dramatic score, like he'd done with *Wait Until Dark*, but he needed more opportunities to do so. One of the early reviews for *The Molly Maguires* was especially encouraging for him in attaining his personal goal of doing more dramatic work. "Showing immense restraint, Mancini never veers into melodrama, but instead, stays true to the culture and the world of the film," it said. *The Molly Maguires* became one of Hank's personal favorites.

It became clear that Hank was in high demand outside of the world of Blake Edwards. That same year he signed on to do the film *Sunflower*, starring Sophia Loren and Marcello Mastroianni. Directed by Vittorio De Sica, it told the story of an Italian woman who, armed only with a photograph of her husband, went on a desperate search to find him after he was considered missing in action in Russia after World War II. It was the first western-produced film to be shot in the USSR. In the Soviet Union, the woman visited the sunflower fields, where there was said to be one flower for every fallen Italian soldier. The "love theme" from the film was sweeping, melancholic, and yet, ultimately tranquil. It encapsulated the idea of inevitability that many of Hank's scores have—that even though we may be surprised by the twists and turns of a story, it ends up completely where it should. This theme and entire score conveyed that by beautifully and poignantly supporting the film's bittersweet ending. Hank cherished the opportunity to write classic Italian-sounding cues, employ Russian folk music, and use a grand romanticism to help tell this story. In 1971, Hank received his fourth Academy Award nomination for Best Score for *Sunflower*, making it his twelfth nomination overall, including nods for Best Song. And once again, he was competing against himself with additional nominations that year for Best Score and Best Song for *Darling Lili*.

Also in 1971, Hank began working with actor and director Paul Newman, whom he had long admired. That year, Newman starred in and directed *Sometimes a Great Notion*. He was resolute about wanting Hank to do the music. Paul was the virtual opposite of Blake in terms of his involvement with the music, and wanted to be part of the entire process, from the spotting session to the final mix. Hank didn't mind this at all when it was an artist with the kind of intelligence and taste Paul Newman had. Set in the timber country of Oregon, the music for *Sometimes a Great Notion* reflected the source music of the environment with its country western songs on jukeboxes and radios. In the rousing piece "Lumber-Jack Blues," Hank created a twangy bluegrass feel with banjos and fiddles. He also collaborated with lyricists Alan and Marilyn Bergman on the ballad "All His Children," which was nominated for an Academy Award. He treasured working with Paul Newman and in the 1980s went on to work with him on the television movie *The Shadow Box* and another feature film, *Harry and Son*.

On their third feature film together, 1987's *The Glass Menagerie*, Paul felt he needed to remind Hank of one of his biggest pet peeves in film scoring.

"Say, Hank," Paul said to him early on. "No damn violins, got it?"

"Well, boss, that's a bit of a strong statement, don't you think?" Hank asked.

"No. I don't want any damn violins."

"You're starting to sound like Howard Hawks, who also told me he didn't want any damn violins."

"Yeah, well, he was right."

"But, Paul, Howard ended up with a few violins."

"Okay, but *we* won't."

Hank felt he needed to soften Paul's stance on this, seeing as how he understood what Paul meant, even though omitting violins wasn't necessarily the best way to achieve what the director wanted. He knew that Paul was really saying that he didn't want it to sound syrupy or schmaltzy, and the best way he knew to express that was just to say *no damn violins*. It is an invaluable skill of the film composer to be able to interpret the words of non-musical collaborators. Hank had no interest in arguing with Paul Newman, as good of friends as they'd become, and figured he would just let the music do the talking. Hank found Paul to be a genuinely admirable guy, and he was impressed by Paul's deep love and appreciation for the talent of his wife, Joanne Woodward. While spotting the music for *The Glass Menagerie*, starring Woodward in the role of the mother, Amanda Wingfield, Paul would sit back in his chair, gaze at her on the screen, and say, "Isn't she something?" Once Hank's score was finished and put into the film, Paul was moved to tears as he watched it. Later, after going over some notes and cuts, Hank felt the need to confess.

"There *are* just a few violins in there," Hank told him.

"Mancini, you scoundrel!"

"But they're deftly disguised by the cellos and violas, wouldn't you say?"

In an interview about the film, Paul described Hank this way: "Henry is certainly a gifted musician and certainly a gentleman. But much more than that, only in the service of the music, and not in the service of Henry Mancini."

There was a silly side of Paul that Hank absolutely adored too. It's why he agreed to accompany Paul and Joanne when they signed for the launch for Paul's brand of spaghetti sauce. Just imagine Hank trying to keep a straight face as Paul sang to the tune of Gershwin's "I've Got Rhythm" at a hamburger shack in Burbank:

I'm as content as I can be
That now I have a spaghetti
Of which my ancestors can be
So justly proud of me
From Sha-ker Heights
To Ve-nice nights
And now Andretti says that he
Would like to give me the Grand Prix
For having finally made a sauce

That's like he had in Italy
He then ran a vic'try lap
For him and me

These were the moments that reminded Hank never to take life too seriously. He knew there was much to be grateful for. It would be an anomaly for anyone who has ever worked in Hollywood to never experience rejection. Hank could have gone his entire career without any, had he not signed on to do a picture with legendary director Alfred Hitchcock.

The film was called *Frenzy*, and though Hank found Hitchcock to be completely pleasant to work with, in the end, the director threw out Hank's score. The situation was seen as ironic by observers, who knew that Hitchcock had become old-fashioned and could no longer appeal to the boomers, which was why Hank was hired in the first place. But Hank had changed and matured too, and wanted to develop his more formal orchestral suspense writing, instead of delivering the lighter suspenseful kind of score as he did on *Charade*. They recorded the score for *Frenzy* in London; Hitchcock nodded the entire time, which Hank took as approval because the director didn't say much of anything. But once the film got to the final mix, Hitchcock decided it wasn't going to work. He never called Hank to discuss this—rather, Hank found out through others involved with the production that Hitchcock found his score too lurid, which made no sense to Hank, considering that it was that kind of movie. This was a bitter pill to swallow, as Hank was never able to truly trace back where their communication had gone wrong. In their early meetings, they seemed to be completely in agreement about the direction and instrumentation.

Still, the way things ended did not change Hank's opinion

of the director and his iconic body of work. Aside from their creative differences, Hitchcock was always incredibly gracious with Hank. He once sent a case of Château Haut-Brion to Hank's office after discovering their mutual love of red wine.

By this time, Hank was becoming very good at juggling the three pins of film scoring, recording albums, and touring. Still under contract with RCA, he was obligated to deliver three albums a year. Perry Como, Elvis, and Harry Belafonte were all on RCA at the time, which was beginning to shift away from the MOR genre that Hank and Perry represented. Hank began to sense this shift when RCA's promotion people continued getting younger and younger and began addressing him as "Mr. Mancini." All told, he had recorded sixty albums in twenty years for the label. He'd kept very busy with recording dates, continuing in his role as a job creator for musicians.

When he found out that his old friend Jack's eldest son, Bruce, a trumpet player, had moved to Los Angeles and had already been working with Doc Severinsen, Hank was excited to bring Bruce in for some session work. He scheduled him for a recording date, and the day before, Bruce passed away at just twenty-one years old. He'd battled severe Crohn's disease most of his life but never let it get in the way of his musical ambitions. Hank's heart shattered for his oldest and dearest friend.

Freddie Dale remained in the position of booking Hank's concerts. Hank had been playing a lot in Japan and Australia, as well as one of the most coveted venues the world over, the Royal Albert Hall in London. Based on Hank's ample library, Freddie was key in procuring an offer for Hank to do his own television show. It was a syndicated show called *The Mancini Generation* that played on over 150 stations around the country. The *Los Angeles Times* called it "a treat for the ear and the eye." The concept included live music, for which Hank assembled an excellent band with many of his regular players and two newcomers in the sax section, who were both Italian—Don Menza and Ray Pizzi. They shot twenty-eight episodes on location at places such as Disneyland and Lion Country Safari. Each episode was designed to showcase the work of a college student who would shoot and edit an original short film set to an existing Mancini recording. The show then awarded scholarships to the winners—yet another way Hank found to support the next generation and film scoring programs in colleges.

Hank delighted in having his good friend and drummer Shelly Manne in this band. Aside from Shelly's musical brilliance, he was one of the funniest musicians Hank had ever worked with. It was customary for Shelly to tell all the latest jokes off the street before they could begin a session. Other times, it was just his lightning-quick wit that broke Hank up, like the time Hank described the very specific kind of feel he was looking for to Shelly.

"Give me 1926," Hank said.

Shelly responded, "Sure. What month?"

Hank originally wanted bassist Ray Brown, with whom he'd worked since the early 1960s, to be in *The Mancini Generation* band. He always fondly remembered one of the first times he saw Ray play with the Oscar Peterson Trio at the LondonHouse in Chicago.

"What a set," Hank told Ray after the show, pumping his hand up and down.

"Thanks, man. Very kind of you," Ray replied. Hank could hear in his voice that he was a bit weary.

"How's everything going out here?"

"It's great. But grueling. You know."

"You wake up and don't know what city you're in?"

"Exactly," Ray said. "I'm about ready to get off the road for a bit. I've been thinking of moving out to Los Angeles, actually."

"No kidding?"

"Do you think it's a good idea?"

"It would certainly be my gain. I sure could use you on my sessions."

Ray stared back at Hank, trying to get a read on how real this offer was. What he didn't realize then was that Hank was a man of his word. Show business was filled with people who made a lot of promises they never intended to keep, so it was natural for Ray to maintain his skepticism after hearing such a thing.

"I mean it. Call me as soon as you get out there, all right?" Hank said.

"I'll do that, Hank."

Hank kept his promise and put Ray to work right away in many of his recordings. In fact, Ray got so busy that he was already booked when it came time to do *The Mancini Generation.* He didn't want to leave Hank in a lurch, so in an ongoing effort to grow the real-world Mancini generation, Ray brought nineteen-year-old bassist John Clayton to Hank's studio to be considered for the job. This was incredibly exciting for such a young and very promising musician. John was wide-eyed as he and Ray entered the recording studio and approached Hank.

"I've heard amazing things about you, John. I'd love to have you aboard," Hank said.

"Mr. Mancini, it's an honor to meet you," John replied.

"Call me Hank."

"Hank. Thank you. Don't you need me to audition? I have my bass . . ."

"That's not necessary. I trust Ray one hundred and ten percent."

"Well, there's one problem . . ." John was a bit flustered, in disbelief that he was in this predicament.

"What's the trouble, son?" Hank asked.

"It's just that . . . I won't be able to work full time because I'm getting ready to go away to college."

"Congratulations! That's wonderful. Where will you be attending?"

John sighed in relief and said, "Indiana University."

"Indiana? Well, that's perfect." Hank looked over at Ray, who already knew the connection. "This show is committed to helping young musicians get established. We'll get you on as many of these as we can before you go and then I'll put you in touch with my contractor, Al Cobine, at Indiana U. That way, you can do some of my concert work too."

The Mancini Generation was very well received and eventually released an album—it was John Clayton's first professional recording. He later went on to co-found the Clayton-Hamilton Jazz Orchestra and reflected on his work with Hank, saying, "Hank did more for musicians than most people realize."

The West Coast editor of *Down Beat* magazine, Harvey Siders, wrote liner notes for *The Mancini Generation*'s album and pointed out that it had been five years since the last Mancini big band recording and that another one was long overdue. He heard and loved all the hard work Hank had put into it, worrying over each and every hemidemisemiquaver—also known as a sixty-fourth note—in the charts. Hank told Siders, "There's so much depth there, it gives me the feeling of infinity."

~

Hank was honored when he was chosen to score the *Visions of Eight* documentary on the 1972 Olympic Games in Munich, Germany. The structure of the film was owed to the title—eight different segments directed by eight directors who represented different countries. Unlike anything Hank had ever done before, it was a great opportunity for him to experiment, which he did to great effect with synthesizers and a palette of other ethereal and otherworldly sounds. In keeping with the sports theme, Los Angeles Rams owner Carroll Rosenbloom asked him to write a new fight song for the team. Hank never thought he would have so much fun debuting and conducting "The Rams are Rollin'" at halftime in the Los Angeles Coliseum.

Indeed, there was much to celebrate. In 1974, Hank turned fifty and Ginny threw him a party of a lifetime. She chose the storied Beverly Hills Hotel for the occasion and planned every detail for the black-tie affair to a T. As soon as Hank entered the ballroom, he knew it was going to be a magical evening. There were people from every aspect and era of his life, including many he hadn't seen in years, like James Cagney, "the First Lady of American Theater" Helen Hayes, and legendary Paramount Pictures film producer A. C. Lyles. Ginny had done a great job not letting Hank in on any of the big surprises of the night. He'd been so overwhelmed at the beginning of the party, hugging and greeting everyone, that it didn't even occur to him that anything was hidden behind the stage curtain. So, when the lights flashed and the drapes were pulled back to reveal the Crystal Room stage, he was absolutely awed to see his old friend and bandleader from his postwar days, Tex Beneke, saluting him.

"Happy birthday, maestro," Tex said into the microphone. Hank's eyes darted around the stage in disbelief—Tex had assembled so many players from the days when Hank and Ginny first met. It was another completely full-circle moment and Hank was incredibly moved. He looked over at Ginny, finding it hard to believe he ever played so hard to get with her. He sometimes felt she could read his thoughts, and this party was no exception.

As the band went into their first song of the night, the Glenn Miller classic "Moonlight Serenade," Hank was overwhelmed. Later in the evening, Chris and the twins gave Hank a warm and humorous tribute. Tony Martin, Mel Torme, and Andy Williams sang an original medley called "Mooncini," and the crowd was all laughs as the great Broadway lyricist Sammy Cahn got up to do his parody of "Moon River."

"Hank, this is for you, friend. Just a reminder not to forget the little people," Sammy said, then began to sing:

Chopped liver
On a piece of rye
That's something I must try, someday
The best pickins
From blessed chickens
If my name is Cohen
I'm goin' your way

Then the moment came that many of the guests knew about, but not Hank. Earlier in the night, Ginny had got up to sing with some of the old Mel-Tones and others. But this time, she took the stage as a solo singer—something she didn't often do with her low alto voice. When she was younger and had auditioned for glee club, she couldn't hit a high note and quickly realized her strength was going to be in harmonizing. She grew to love being what she called "the hot note in the middle." For this occasion, however, there was no need for any voice other than her own as she serenaded Hank with the song "What Are You Doing the Rest of Your Life?"

I want to see your face in every kind of light
In fields of dawn and forests of the night
And when you stand before the candles on a cake
Oh, let me be the one to hear the silent wish you make

What are you doing the rest of your life?
North and South and East and West of your life
I have only one request of your life
That you spend it all with me

All the seasons and the times of your days
All the nickels and the dimes of your days
Let the reasons and the rhymes of your days
All begin and end with me

Those tomorrows waiting deep in your eyes
In the world of love that you keep in your eyes
I'll awaken what's asleep in your eyes
It may take a kiss or two

Through all of my life
Summer, winter, spring, and fall of my life
All I ever will recall of my life
Is all of my life with you

Ginny's performance promptly vaporized Hank into a virtual puddle on the floor. The fact that this song was written by their friends Alan and Marilyn Bergman made it all the more special. Hank turned to the others at his table and said, "I suppose it's fitting this song was written for a movie called *The Happy Ending*. Thank you, everyone. Thank you all for being here."

The gaping hole in the guest list, of course, was Blake. After all the years of not speaking with Blake, Hank spotted him one day from the balcony of his and Ginny's rented house in Malibu. Hank called out to him and, at first, he wasn't certain if Blake was going to stop. He rushed outside to get down to where Blake was on the beach.

"Blake! Blake, can we please talk a minute?" Hank asked.

Finally, Blake stopped, deciding to hear him out.

"Listen," Hank said, catching his breath. "I'd really like to be able to put any bad feelings behind us. I don't know if you realize what the studio was up to, but my only part in it is being too damn naïve. I didn't fully appreciate the old divide-and-conquer strategy until I got caught up in it."

Blake stared back at him. He was still holding on to a lot of bitterness, but perhaps in that moment he realized it was wrongly directed at Hank, who continued:

"I'm sorry for everything that happened during *Darling Lili*. It's a fine piece of work that I'm proud to have done with you. I apologize for anything I did or didn't do. It pains me to think you would believe I'd ever do anything to undermine you. I could never have conjured up a better partner than you," Hank said.

"Our director-composer relationship is rivaled *only* by Alfred Hitchcock and Bernard Hermann," Blake offered.

Hank smiled.

"So, why stop now?" Blake asked.

Then, just like that, they straightened out all their misunderstandings—just in time for them to soon do a sequel to *The Pink Panther*, twelve years after the original. Ginny looked on from the balcony and sighed and smiled.

Chapter Thirteen

RECYCLED JOY

The Mancini Generation was, of course, more than just the name of a television show and continued to expand in new and unexpected ways. *The Return of the Pink Panther* in 1975 introduced a whole new generation to the music of Henry Mancini. This came as a complete shock to Hank, because it had been a decade since the sequel to *The Pink Panther*—the oddly titled *A Shot in the Dark,* named after the stage play it was based on—had been released. Blake Edwards never seriously considered continuing the franchise beyond his first two Panther films, especially considering that the third installment, entitled *Inspector Clouseau,* was universally panned, perhaps partly due to the fact that neither Blake nor Hank worked on it. Edwards had in fact written a fifteen- to twenty-page treatment shortly after *A Shot in the Dark,* but when it failed to develop beyond those initial pages, he turned his creative efforts elsewhere. Then, rather suddenly, there was renewed interest from financiers about resurrecting the property, and United Artists called a meeting to discuss the possibility of a new film starring the lovable and bumbling Inspector Clouseau.

The old adage "timing is everything" was surely a factor in terms of this coming together because another Pink Panther movie would not have been possible without Mancini's music, which was seen as part of the franchise's DNA. For Hank, this follow-up film turned out to be a much different assignment from the first two. Times had changed a great deal in the decade between those films and this new one. Audiences were now accustomed to broader comedy with bigger effects and outrageous stunts, even when they did little to enhance the story. Hank had to make his music fit this new mold, which required a different tone than the slinky, sly cocktail music of the first two movies. This new iteration was over the top and cartoonish, but Hank's score once again brought great value to it.

The term "filmharmonic" was coined around this time to describe performances like those put on by the Henry Mancini Orchestra that showcased symphonic performances of film scores. Hank had truly come into his own as a conductor and now thoroughly enjoyed performing live. He was more astonished about this than anyone, considering how much he used to loathe performing publicly, going back to being that kid in the Sons of Italy band.

As soon as he booked an engagement in Cleveland for the orchestra, he knew he wanted to make sure Jack would be there. Hank was not surprised in the least when he called to invite him and found out that Jack had already purchased his own tickets for the show. Hank told him to be sure to come backstage after the show at the large outdoor Blossom Center—an architectural band shell in the middle of the woods in Cuyahoga Falls. It was such a joy for Jack to hear the Henry Mancini Orchestra—and on a warm summer night under the stars, it was even more magical.

The orchestra played through several Mancini favorites and Jack, having followed Hank's career so closely, knew the concert program was always being updated with different tunes. Hank enjoyed doing new arrangements of other people's songs, both old and new. The Mancini catalog was unlike any other in that it had something for everyone. As one of Hank's Italian players used to say, Hank's concerts were always *allegrezza*, which means "joyful" in Italian. It was important to him that his musicians enjoy themselves as much as the audience and he was always acknowledging them, telling crowds that he would be nowhere without them. Al Cobine never had any trouble getting the best musicians across the country to play these dates with Hank. Al once said, "Hank was so loyal. Of all the big stars, I never knew of one who treated his sidemen so well."

Halfway through the show in Cleveland, Hank went to the microphone.

"Good evening, Cleveland," he said. "I hope you are enjoying yourselves and having a wonderful time. I know we are up here. It's a joy to present these songs for you and we'd like to thank you for being here with us tonight. I'd like to just take a moment to acknowledge a very important person who is in the crowd tonight. He is my oldest friend and we grew up together in good ol' West Aliquippa, PA. Oh, the mischief we would get up to! His name is John Weitzel. Jack, where are you? Please stand up, Jack."

The crowd began to applaud as Hank searched the audience for his old pal.

"I'd like to acknowledge Jack," Hank continued, "not just for being such a great friend but, more importantly, for the phenomenal work he's been doing as director of the Aviator Marching Band at Alliance High School, just down the road from here. Jack and I have enjoyed our own alliance for so many years now, and the work he's doing with these young people is just tremendous. They've been playing halftime shows at Cleveland Browns games and Detroit Lions games, and now the Football Hall of Fame parade. They're going to have to build a new wing onto the school for all their trophies. So, I salute you, Jack. And go Aviators!"

The spotlight operator located Jack in the crowd and Hank gave him a salute. For Jack, this was the moment of a lifetime. He nodded, mouthing the words "thank you" to Hank and to everyone around him. Jack was like family to Hank, and Jack knew how much Hank recognized the value of family. Hank had never been one to take anything for granted, but after seeing the strength and grace Jack exhibited after losing his son, he counted his blessings with even more frequency.

In 1976, Chris came to Hank and Ginny with some news. His longtime girlfriend, Julie, whom he'd met at school in Arizona and had subsequently moved to California, was expecting a baby. Hank and Ginny were absolutely thrilled to become grandparents and overjoyed to welcome Christopher Michael Mancini. The young couple kept the baby for a year, but they struggled. Being such young parents, they were unprepared for the demands of parenthood. Hank and Ginny discussed over a glass of wine one night what they could do to help them.

"It's clear to me that Chris needs more time to get himself established," Hank said.

"Yes, that is clear," Ginny agreed. Her instinct was to give young Chris the best because they had all they needed to do so, and all the love in the world for their darling grandson. "I think maybe Chris Jr. should come and live with us," she said.

"Are you sure you want to take that on?"

"I can't stand to think of him not getting everything he needs, especially in his formative years, Henry. Think of it like the way they do things in the old world—a bit like an extended family situation."

"Let's talk to Chris and Julie and make sure it's what they want too."

They invited the young couple over with the baby for Sunday dinner. Bouncing her grandson on her lap, Ginny broached the subject.

"Your dad and I have been thinking about this—we know how difficult it has been for you two, trying to get yourselves established, working on your own relationship, and parenting," she said. "It's not easy! We always thought we'd have more children, and after the twins arrived we realized we had just the right amount."

Julie reached across the table to wiggle a rattle in front of the baby. "We love him so much," she said, a hint of sadness in her voice.

It was as though everyone already knew where this conversation was heading.

"If you two think it would be a help to you, we would like to have Chris Jr. live with us for a while until you both have your feet underneath you," Ginny said.

"What do you think?" Hank asked them.

Chris and Julie looked at each other and silently agreed.

"I think it might be a good idea," Chris said.

"Okay," Julie echoed, feeling a mixed bag of emotions.

Ginny went right to work remaking Felice's old bedroom into a nursery for Chris Jr., and they hired a nanny to help. At fifty-two, Hank and Ginny had begun to enjoy their empty nest and were now giving up their freedom all over again. In the blink of an eye they were parents once more, tripping over toys and baby gear scattered throughout the house.

The upside, of course, was little blond Chris Jr., who was pure bliss. Hank and Ginny took him everywhere. In a letter to Jack and Dixie, Hank referred to Chris Jr. as "a constant source of recycled joy." This was also a good way to describe this period of Hank's life, as film sequels and touring continued to pay off, despite seeing younger composers getting films he would have liked to do. He accepted this as the normal progression of things and had been working very hard throughout his career to ensure that the next generation would have the tools they needed to succeed in scoring motion pictures. He was revered in every corner of the business and it was a good time to be focusing on his family.

In his ongoing effort to give back and educate, Hank agreed to teach a seminar at the American Film Institute in Los Angeles. For the occasion, he selected three clips of his work from the films *The Great Race*, *The White Dawn*, and *A Touch of Evil.* When the projectionist put up the first clip from *A Touch of Evil,* the normally unflappable Hank became very perturbed.

"Hold it, hold it. Where did this come from?" Hank asked.

The audience could see that he was flustered.

"Mr. Mancini, sir, we arranged to get it on loan from the studio. It was sent over by them, one of the students said."

"Where have they been keeping the print? In the walk-in at the studio commissary between the meat and the cheese?"

Some laughed to break the tension, but Hank was not finding any of it funny.

"Forgive me, I'm just appalled that they could do this to Orson's work," he said.

One of the coordinators of the event stood up and said, "We're very sorry, Mr. Mancini. We only want your work presented in the best possible way."

"I'm not worried about me. This is Orson's legacy we're talking about."

A faculty member tried to pivot while another clip was being loaded onto the projector. "Mr. Mancini, we have a question over here," he pointed out.

"Call me Hank, *pleeease*."

A young man stood up to ask his question. "I'm just curious," he said. "I don't know if you can really even answer this, but . . ."

"I'll certainly try," Hank said.

"Well, I mean . . . you've been nominated for seventy-two Grammys and won twenty, nominated for seventeen Oscars, won three. Recorded eighty-five albums, eight of them Gold. Two Emmy nominations, a Golden Globe nomination, a Lifetime Grammy Achievement Award, and four honorary degrees. And your classic theme you wrote for *The Pink Panther* became an animated cartoon series that will probably run forever."

This was not even the final tally of Hank's awards and honors.

"You have all that memorized?" Hank laughed incredulously.

"So, my question is, how is it that every time you go to score something you come up with something entirely delightful, charming, and unexpected?"

Some giggled at the earnestness of the question.

"Oh, that's an easy one," Hank said.

The crowd sat up straighter in their seats as if they were about to receive a priceless pearl of wisdom from a master.

"I'm Italian on both sides."

The audience laughed as the young man pursued a follow-up question. "Okay, just take *The Pink Panther* theme as an example. How did you come up with that?"

"What else would you write for a pink panther?" Hank laughed. "It's like Alfred Newman always says, 'Don't tell the same joke twice.' If the visual is humorous, the way a pink panther is inherently humorous, you've got to do something musically to counter that, give it some gravitas. You want to leave something between the eye and the ear so that the audience can use some of their own imagination to fill in that space."

The evening was going to be okay after all, though Hank was exasperated to see that the second clip was almost as damaged as the first one.

"Oh, so it was no accident. They really are storing these in the meat locker," he said. "Well, this'll be show-and-tell without the show."

"Mr. Mancini. Excuse me, I mean, Hank . . ." a young academic in the first row began.

"Yes, sir?"

"Speaking of how badly these films have been archived, I'm just wondering how you feel about the shift of everything to digital. Would you ever consider working that way instead of writing out all your scores longhand?"

"My wife would never let me bring one of those iron lungs into the house!" He continued, "No, I'll keep my process the way it's always been for however long I keep doing this. It's worked for me pretty well. Which reminds me of something I always like to point out in these forums: do this only if you love it. Don't do it for the money, because there's no guarantee you'll make any. If you want to make money in music, get into the marching band uniform business. I mean that sincerely."

Hank continued to do wildly different films. His next one with Blake was among the year's biggest box office hits: *10*, starring Dudley Moore and Bo Derek. It was particularly amusing for Hank to work on, because Moore's character was a composer in the midst of a midlife crisis. He knew that, like much of Blake's work, it was autobiographical, and Blake couldn't very well have made it about a film director without it being entirely too close to home.

Hank found immense satisfaction that the movie brought renewed fame to the classical piece *Boléro*, by Maurice Ravel. The exposure from the film resulted in massive sales for the song, which was still under copyright at the time and generated $1 million in royalties, briefly making Ravel the time's bestselling classical composer forty years after his death. Of course, many people assumed Hank had written it.

"Sure," he would joke, "Along with the *William Tell* overture and 'The Star-Spangled Banner.'"

Orion Pictures, the studio, wanted Blake to do a disco version of *Boléro*. Mercifully, Blake flat-out refused, trying to explain that the classical music was what made its accompanying scene so hilarious.

On the absolute other end of the spectrum, Hank was hired to score *Mommie Dearest*, the controversial story written by Christina Crawford, the daughter of Joan Crawford, about her life growing up as the star's daughter. Most critics of *Mommie Dearest* agreed that Hank's score was the only element of the melodrama that bothered to analyze the psychology of the characters beyond the surface level. His music was described as "intimate, thoughtful, confiding, and cautionary." Hank felt it wasn't simply the tale of a madwoman but, perhaps more accurately, a lost woman. He found the humanity in Joan, played by Faye Dunaway, even though the music seemed to focus more on the perspective of her tortured but forgiving daughter. The soft score managed to make the audience feel safe despite all the psychological and physical danger onscreen.

After that rather intense experience, Hank was relieved to return to comedy for his next picture, *Victor/Victoria*, another project with Blake and Julie Andrews. Hank soon came to believe it was one of the most perfect films he'd ever been involved with. In the gender-bending farce, Julie played a struggling entertainer in 1930s Paris, who was saved by a cabaret performer with a big idea—that she become a male impersonator pretending to be a female impersonator. Soon her character became the toast of the town.

The project was an opportunity for Hank to bring together all his skills in composing, songwriting, and writing for the visual medium in a way he'd never done before. He partnered with lyricist Leslie Bricusse, to whom Sammy Davis Jr. had introduced him years earlier at the Mayfair Hotel in London, where Hank's suite had come with a piano—Sammy had asked if he and Leslie could use it for a little while, and Hank then witnessed Leslie's incredible talent up close.

Before *Victor/Victoria*, he'd worked with Leslie once before on *Two for the Road*. Leslie's first love was musical theater, and at times it seemed to Hank that Leslie knew absolutely everything about every musical ever written. For Hank, *Victor/Victoria* was just one of those films where everything came together in cinematic alchemy, and it became one of the only films of his he could watch over and over. Although the film received seven Academy Award nominations across various categories, the only people who went home that night with Oscars for it were Hank and Leslie for Best Score.

As strange as the 1980s were for the film and music businesses, the decade ended up being good to Hank. In 1984, he recorded the album *In the Pink* with Irish flautist James Galway in London. They had first met the year before at the Grammy Awards, when Hank was backstage at the Shrine Auditorium near the dressing rooms and heard someone playing *The Pink Panther* on flute. James and his wife, Jeanne, became dear friends of Hank and Ginny. Hank described James as "one of the most open, honest, and loving people I've ever met. His only fault is that he's not Italian."

Hank was inducted into the Songwriter's Hall of Fame in 1984 and proudly watched his son, Chris, make a very solid rock album with Atlantic Records. Chris was incredibly talented and proficient on all the new synthesizers, which was a great help to Hank when he needed to incorporate new digital sounds into his palette. Hank was proud of Chris's musical talent, but when the album didn't break through, he thought Chris might have more success in another area of the music business. He introduced him to some contacts he had at Arista Records in the music publishing department, where Chris's career began in earnest.

In a return to television, Hank scored the critically acclaimed mini-series *The Thorn Birds*. The series was based on the bestselling epic novel of the same name by Australian author Colleen McCullough, and it became one of the highest-rated mini-series of the time, second only to *Roots*. Hank's approach to this score was elegant and understated. He took much of his inspiration from the mythical thorn bird referenced in the title—a bird that sings just once in its life, but sings the most beautiful song the world has ever heard.

In 1982, Hank had an engagement at the Hollywood Bowl. Ginny invited a group of friends to join her for his performance and packed gourmet picnic baskets for them, a tradition at the Bowl. The group met at the Mancini residence and Ginny "expertly" parked all the guests' cars in a highly organized fashion so that there was enough room for all of them—then they rode over to the venue in rented limousines so people could safely celebrate the night out with wine and champagne. Chris Jr. was only six and Hank wanted to stay back and have dinner with him before leaving to go to his show. Chris had an early bedtime and, as much as he would have enjoyed the performance, he would have been asleep on Ginny's lap after the first couple songs.

When Hank finished dinner and turned Chris over to the babysitter, he found he couldn't get *his* car out of the garage, as it was barricaded in by all the other cars. Just as he began to panic, the twins drove up.

"Dad, aren't you supposed to be at the Hollywood Bowl?" Monica asked.

"That's the idea, yeah. Except that your mother blocked me in with all these other cars."

The twins started laughing in their eerie stereo fashion.

"Hop in, Dad. We'll give you a lift," Felice told him.

"Oh, how kind of you," he said with a wink.

"You got your baton and everything?" Monica asked.

"Very funny," he muttered, climbing into the backseat.

It wasn't until she was backstage after the show that Ginny found out what chaos she'd caused. The group went into the dressing room and began congratulating Hank on a wonderful show.

"Bravo, maestro!" they cheered.

"That was wonderful, Hank. Thank you for inviting us," someone said.

"Well, it almost didn't happen," he said.

"How do you mean?" someone asked.

"You see, Chris Jr. and I were enjoying our lovely dinner of *fettuccine Bolognese* and *insalata mista*, discussing the finer points of his Lego rocket ship, when I figured I'd better get my rear in gear. So, I got down to the garage and what did I find? All your very expensive cars blocking mine! Now, I could have had my pick of many fine automobiles to joyride in, if only I had the keys!"

Ginny howled with nervous laughter. "Did I really do that?"

Hank turned to their friends and said, "Normally, she's quite deft with all the details!"

By late 1986, Ginny's mother, Jo, no longer wanted to travel with the family for the holidays. Hank, Ginny, the kids, and Chris Jr. went to Vail for Christmas to ski and Jo stayed at home in Malibu. One night, her electric blanket caught fire. Her long-time housekeeper was able to pull her out of the fire, but not before she sustained second- and third-degree burns. The family returned to Los Angeles immediately, and Hank and Ginny went straight to the hospital where Jo was in the intensive care unit.

"I'm terrified to see her this way, Henry," Ginny said, steeling herself before going through the door to Jo's room. He squeezed her hand.

"I'm here. C'mon," he said, opening the door.

Ginny went to her mother's side and sat down next to her bed. It was heartbreaking to see her in such pain. A nurse came over.

"*Estoy en tanto dolor, mija,*" Jo said, barely making out the words.

Ginny turned to the nurse, tears filling her eyes. "She says she's in terrible pain. Isn't there more we can do for her?"

"With her weight at eighty pounds, we can't give her painkillers," the nurse said.

"Well, that doesn't make any sense," Hank said, hating to see both his wife and her mother in this state.

"I'd like to speak to her doctor," Ginny said.

"He's in surgery now," the nurse said.

"Then as soon as he's out." Ginny stood over her mother to gently embrace her. She whispered in her ear. "I'm so sorry, Mama. This should never have happened."

Hours later, the doctor came by to check on Jo. When he finished examining her, Ginny asked to speak to him in the hallway. Hank went with her.

"Doctor, we appreciate everything you're doing for her, but she's suffering horribly," Ginny said. "Why can't you give her anything for the pain?"

"We could, but then she would lose the functions that are keeping her alive," he explained.

Ginny began to get upset.

"I'm very sorry," the doctor told them.

They continued to stay by Jo's side for the next week.

"If they won't give me pain medicine, how about some champagne?" Jo asked in Spanish.

Ginny had to giggle through her tears. She turned to Hank. "She wants champagne."

"You've come to the right guy," Hank said, happy that there was something he could do. "It's New Year's Eve, after all."

Hank returned with a couple of bottles of very expensive bubbly. "Only the best for my Jo," he said as he presented them.

Ginny pulled Hank aside. "She told me she doesn't think she can go on. She wants to be taken off life support."

This hit Hank hard. But he knew he needed to be strong for his wife and for Jo. "If that's what you both think is best," he said.

He popped the cork and poured three glasses into paper cups. They stayed with Jo all night, and on New Year's Day Hank opened the second bottle of champagne. As they finished it off, Jo was unhooked from life support and slipped away. According to Jo's wishes, Hank and Ginny scattered her ashes over the Pacific Ocean.

In the summer of 1987, Hank embarked on a new recording project, *Volare*, with Luciano Pavarotti, their second recording project together. Three years earlier they'd done an album called *Mamma* that became a worldwide success and for which they gave a Royal Variety Performance to Queen Elizabeth. *Volare* was to be recorded in Bologna, Italy. Hank decided to bring Ginny and Chris Jr., whom Hank felt should see Italy as it was part of his heritage. One weekend during the project, Luciano invited the three of them to his seaside country home in Pesaro, overlooking the Adriatic Sea. Luciano and Chris Jr., then ten years old, became fast friends when Luciano offered him an extra bicycle to ride alongside him as he biked around the villa for his daily exercise. Chris Jr. absolutely loved this, and it seemed to bring out the child in Pavarotti.

Chris Jr. had a deep love of animals. One morning at the villa, he was out exploring when he came upon a baby bird that had fallen out of its nest. Hank watched from the window as Chris carefully picked it up off the ground, then he went outside to meet him.

"What did you find there, Christopher?" he asked.

"Papa, it's a baby bird. It's still alive but it can't fly," Chris said.

"What can we do?"

"Can we put it in a box? And find some food for it?"

"Sure, son. Let's go see."

Luciano's cook gave them a box and suggested an eyedropper to feed the bird sugar water. For the next two days, Chris Jr. looked over the baby bird, feeding it, talking to it, and taking it outside for fresh air. He was so determined to save the creature's life. On day three, he awoke to find that the bird had not survived the night. He grew teary-eyed as he took it to the kitchen, where he found Hank and Luciano.

"*Buongiorno*, Christopher," Luciano said with gusto. Then he noticed Chris staring down into the box, his shoulders slumped.

"The baby bird flew all the way to heaven last night," Chris said matter-of-factly.

"Oh, Christopher. I am sorry. I know he was your friend," Luciano said.

"Do you have a glass jar for me to bury him?"

"*Si, si, si.* Of course, my boy." He opened a cupboard and took out a glass for canning with a metal lid. "Here you are," Luciano said, handing it to him.

"And a paper and pencil so I can write a note to put inside with him?" Chris asked.

Hank and Luciano watched as Chris went outside to a patch of woods behind the villa to bury the jar. Luciano was very moved by the whole thing.

"What an incredibly sweet child, Enrico," he said.

The following year, in 1987, Hank was invited to conduct the Pittsburgh Symphony Orchestra. Almost as soon as he touched down on Pennsylvania soil, he felt an unmistakable tug luring him back to West Aliquippa. One of his traveling companions was author Gene Lees, who had begun working with Hank on his autobiography. Hank told Gene and his musician friends that he wanted to rent a car.

"I'm thinking of making a drive out to my hometown to see how it's getting along. I don't really want to make the side trip solo," Hank said.

"What's a side trip without your sidemen?" the guys joked. "We'd love to tag along and see where it all started out for you, Hank."

Hank drove the group in a rented Lincoln along the

Allegheny River and then the Ohio River from Pittsburgh to West Aliquippa. Ohio River Boulevard sat high on the riverbank and offered sweeping views. Hank filled them in on his little hometown.

"Like so many of the towns in this part of the world, it used to be a thriving steel town," he said. "Jones and Laughlin Steel Company employed my father and almost every other man of working age back then. The mill's been closed for a few years now. It was all immigrant families, very hard-working people."

They crossed the bridge over train tracks into West Aliquippa.

"For a time, it was in *Ripley's Believe It or Not!* for being the only town with only one way in and one way out."

"I guess that would be good for people who get lost a lot," one of the guys said.

They all chuckled, but Hank was the first to stop laughing when he saw what was left of the town. They could hear the tires rolling over broken glass as a feral cat darted in front of the car.

"I think it's a few more blocks this way," Hank said. "But nothing looks like it used to. Wait a minute . . . It's on a corner, so it must be down here. So many of the numbers have fallen off of the houses," he said with sadness in his voice.

They finally found it, 401—his childhood home. Hank got out of the car, walked to the house, and sat down on the front steps. He let out an audible sigh as he looked around the completely decimated neighborhood.

"You okay, boss?" someone asked.

"I've never been so flooded with so many memories all at once," he said.

"Anything you can share?" Gene asked.

"There was an actual flood. I was sitting in this exact spot watching whole houses float downriver with animals clinging to the roofs for dear life. It almost wiped out the whole town." He looked around, continuing to survey the scene. "The silence around here is deafening. All you used to hear was the sound of kids playing in the street."

They returned to the car and drove back the way they came, passing a boarded-up building on the main street.

"That used to be the old Sons of Italy Hall," Hank told them, "where I'd go with my father every Sunday after mass to rehearse and get my ration of Puccini."

"Hank, did you ever consider that you could be Puccini reincarnated? You were born right after he died, you know," Gene pointed out.

"That's funny you say that, Gene. When I was in the army, a psychic told me I was the reincarnation of Verdi. So, which one is it?"

The car was split on this point.

"Hey, do you all mind if I go by my high school?" Hank asked. "I'm not really sure if it's even there anymore. It doesn't seem like there are enough people here to keep a high school open."

"Let's go find out," someone said.

They turned out of West Aliquippa and headed to Main Street of Aliquippa proper. Hank pulled up in front of the school.

"Hey, the doors are open," Hank said. "That's promising."

The group got out of the car and approached the entrance. They went inside, where Hank found his way to the music room. It was unlocked. He pushed the door open and right away his eyes were drawn to the little spinet piano in the corner of the room. It was a smaller and much less expensive model than a regular piano. He floated over to it, as if in a dream, and hovered his hands over it.

"This is the same one I used to play when I was a student here," he said.

Just then, the door of the classroom opened and a woman who worked at the school entered.

"Can I help you gentlemen?" she asked.

One of the guys addressed her. "My friend here used to go to this school and he wanted to look around," he said.

"And who is your friend?" she asked skeptically.

"Henry Mancini."

At first she started to laugh, as though they were trying to kid her. And then she noticed the tall Italian man standing beside the piano.

"Henry? Is that really you?" she asked. "We graduated together!" She could barely contain her excitement and wanted to know what in the world ever brought him back to Aliquippa.

"I'm conducting the Pittsburgh Symphony," he said.

She clutched her heart. "Of course you are. Now wait right here. There's something I've got to show you."

She came back a few minutes later with a yearbook. She flipped through it until she found Hank's senior class picture and read what was written next to it.

"'One day I hope to be an arranger and maybe have my own band,'" she read and then looked up at him.

Hank laughed. "And here they are!"

"And he's not just an arranger anymore either," Gene said with a smile.

As difficult as it had been to see his old town in the state it was in, Hank and the guys left Aliquippa on a very high note. Still feeling nostalgic, Hank was excited to drive by the site of the old Stanley Theatre, where he'd studied with Max Adkins. He had thought the Stanley had been torn down, but found out from someone in town that it had undergone a multimillion-dollar renovation and was now the Benedum Center, a venue for opera and musical theater. They went to check it out.

As they had a look around, Hank asked someone on the staff there how to get to the basement, where he used to take his lessons with Max.

"I'm sorry, Mr. Mancini. The old basement is no longer there after the restructuring of the building," the young man told him.

Hank was crestfallen. "And the Loew's Penn? When did they tear that down?"

He was referring to another grand theater of old Pittsburgh, the one he'd gone to as a child with his father to see *The Crusades* all those years ago. "I wish I had known they were going to destroy it. Maybe I could have helped save it."

"The Loew's Penn wasn't torn down, sir. It was completely restored by the H. J. Heinz Company."

"You mean the Heinz Hall, where I'm conducting tomorrow tonight?"

"Yes. That's the old Loew's."

And with that news, Hank felt more recycled joy than he could describe. He turned to his friends and said, "That's where I saw *The Crusades* and first decided I wanted to write music for the movies!"

"So, you'll be conducting on that very stage?" Gene asked, trying to take all this in.

Hank felt tears come to his eyes. It had been a very fruitful roots trip.

Chapter Fourteen

CROSSING IN STYLE

Looking back, it seemed to Hank that he had indeed experienced many serendipitous events in his life. But one of the best was yet to come. For most of their lives together, he and Ginny had dreamed of going on a game-watching safari in Africa. Chris Jr. had already acquired an impressive number of stamps in his passport as a result of his travels with his grandparents, which he enjoyed just as much as they did. By the time he'd turned ten, Christopher had visited more countries than Hank had by age forty. In 1988, Hank and Ginny decided the time had come to journey to Kenya with their young companion for the adventure of a lifetime.

Hank hired a guide, a Kenyan man of Scandinavian descent, named Tor Allen. For their first night, the travelers were put up at a British Colonial–style hotel in the heart of the capital city of Nairobi with crisp white linens, wooden shutters, and lots of potted palms and hanging ferns. The safari would begin the following day at the Lewa Wildlife Conservancy, near Meru

National Park, one of the least visited of all the national parks in Kenya, and the least spoiled. The equator bisects the park, which covers over 1,100 square miles. Meru had become somewhat famous after the 1966 film *Born Free*, about the orphaned lioness named Elsa who was hand-raised by animal conservationist Joy Adamson. It was Joy's wish to be buried next to Elsa and this grave is marked with a plaque next to Adamson's Falls for visitors.

Tor and his wife, Sue, who operated the safari company, worked with a team of a half dozen Maasai tribesmen to set up camp for the expedition, for which they erected a small village. Hank and Ginny were given their own tent complete with shower, private tents were made up for Christopher and Tor, and there was even a separate cooking tent and dining tent. Their days would begin very early, when the wildlife was most active, by gathering for tea and biscuits and then heading straight out to the bush at the break of dawn.

Christopher, the animal lover, planned to keep a list of all the animals he saw. He couldn't believe how quickly he was writing down leopards, cheetahs, elephants, lions, zebras, and hippos. Meru National Park has hundreds of species of birds alone, and Chris got an especially big kick out of seeing a stunning bird made up of several shades of blue stripes hitching a ride on a rhinoceros.

"Are they friends, Papa? They must be friends," he said.

Hank and Ginny both smiled.

"They must be," Hank told him.

"They have what is called a symbiotic relationship," Tor told Chris. "That just means they help each other out in some way. The bird eats bugs off the back of the rhino and the rhino gives the bird a safe place to land."

"So, they can talk to each other?" Chris asked excitedly.

"Not exactly. But they do communicate. Just not with words," Tor told him.

They could all see the gears of Christopher's brain fully engaged as he processed the idea of communication without words.

From Meru, they journeyed north through the savannah of the Shaba game reserve, then west to a fishing camp on the shore of Lake Victoria, where they took a boat out for the day.

"Christopher, did you know this lake is so big that it borders three different countries?" Hank asked.

"Kenya and what other ones?" Christopher asked.

Hank opened the map to show him. "See here?" Hank said, pointing.

Christopher sounded them out. "Uh-ganda?"

"It's a long U sound. Like *you*," Ginny told him.

"Oh. Uganda and Rrrrwww?"

"Rwanda."

"Ra-wan-da," Christopher repeated after Hank.

They cast their lines, and Hank seemed to be charming the fish with no problem. As the day went on, Christopher grew slightly frustrated that he wasn't catching anything. Then, suddenly, he felt a tug.

"Papa, I've got one on the line!"

"Wow! That looks like a biggie, Chris!"

The fish began to give Christopher a real fight.

"Do you want some help with that, Chris?" Tor asked.

Christopher grunted and groaned. "Yes . . ." He struggled with all his might. "Please!"

Tor joined the fight and helped bring in the giant Nile perch. When they arrived back at the dock, they weighed it on a scale.

"Forty-six pounds!" Tor announced. "That's the biggest catch of the day, Christopher!"

The boy smiled, quite pleased with himself. "How much do *I* weigh?" he asked.

"You're about seventy pounds," Ginny told him.

Tor took the fish off the scale and held it up next to Christopher. "The fish is almost as tall as you are too. Here," Tor said, handing over the perch. "Hold him up for a picture." Tor snapped what became one their favorite shots of the entire trip.

That night back at camp, Hank heard something in the distance. He listened closely and followed the sound to the cooking tent, where the cooks were singing as they prepared dinner. He poked his head into the tent and one of them turned to face him.

"Your dinner will be ready soon, Mr. Mancini," the cook said. "Would you like something to eat now?"

"Oh, no, thank you. I just heard your singing. It's wonderful. I had to come closer to hear it better."

"That is very kind of you."

"Would you mind if I record it?" Hank asked, holding up a small tape recorder.

"No problem, Mr. Mancini."

"Great! Thank you. Just pretend I'm not here," he said with a smile, and pushed the record button as they went back to their cooking and singing.

Each evening at sundown, Maasai warriors guarded the camp. They wore tribal dress and held long staffs as they stood lookout for hyenas or other animals attracted to the smell of food. Hank approached them before retiring for the evening.

"I wanted to thank you for looking out for us and taking such good care of us," he said.

"Of course, you are very welcome," one of the warriors said in perfect English.

"Your voices are so marvelous and I've been thoroughly enjoying all the singing people do here," Hank said. "The music and the Maa language is truly enchanting. I listened to the cooks singing earlier tonight and I was wondering if you would you consider joining our campfire tomorrow night and singing something?"

The two warriors looked at each other and one told him, "We will return tomorrow night to sing for you and bring friends."

"You will? Great! I look forward to it." Hank said.

The next night, the two men returned to the camp as promised with two other Maasai. They sang some of their tribe's songs for Hank, Ginny, and Christopher. Hank was moved by the raw power of their voices. Christopher watched and listened attentively, in a dreamlike state. The following day while in the Maasai Mara game reserve, Hank kept thinking about *Hatari!* He'd been meaning to ask Tor about it since they'd arrived.

"Say, Tor, do you happen to know where the film *Hatari!* was shot?"

Tor slowed the jeep to turn to look at him.

"Is something wrong?" Hank asked.

"No, no. It's just that we're headed there right now. You gave me goose bumps is all!" Tor said.

"That's a wild coincidence," Hank replied.

"Most Africans don't believe in coincidence. They either see the hand of God, or the hand of the *other* in everything. To me, you were just meant to come here. Today."

Hank mulled this over in his mind. He turned to the back seat where Ginny and Christopher were and said, "It was meant to be!"

"I'll say! Somebody up there really loves you," Ginny said, gazing up at the vast sky above them.

"Can you believe *Hatari!* was twenty-five years ago already?"

"You mean, I wasn't even born yet?" Christopher asked.

"Can you imagine a time before Christopher?" Ginny said, putting her arm around him.

They arrived at the location where the rhino hunt in the movie had been staged in the film. As the four of them got out of the jeep, Hank felt as though he was stepping into the movie. Tor began greeting people in the village and introduced Hank as the person who'd written the music for *Hatari!*

"My sister and my aunt and cousin all worked on that movie!" one man said.

"Is that right?" Hank asked incredulously.

"Papa, this looks like the trail where the baby elephants walked to the watering hole," Christopher said.

One of the villagers pointed in another direction and said, "No, that is actually a little way over there. Would you like to see it?"

"Can we, Papa?" Christopher asked.

"Of course! Let's go," Hank said.

After they visited the famous watering hole, Tor took them into a factory where women were weaving rugs and were also, of course, singing.

"Would it be all right if I record you?" Hank asked. They were a bit shy at first, but after a few minutes, they started getting into it. Their voices grew louder and louder until they began dancing right out of the factory! It was a full-blown celebration of life that Hank, Ginny, and Christopher had never witnessed anywhere in the world before. When they finished dancing, Tor had a thought.

"Can I play some of Hank's music for you?" he asked the women.

They nodded enthusiastically and followed Tor over to the jeep, where he popped in a cassette Hank didn't even know he had with him. The first song that came on was the theme from *Peter Gunn.* The women began to smile and sway along to the music. When the song ended, they clapped politely. But the next song that came on was "Baby Elephant Walk," and they spontaneously began to dance. One of the men who was watching broke out in an elaborate improvisation that was quite inspired.

That night around the campfire, Hank reached for Christopher and Ginny's hands and, looking up at the star-filled sky, said, "Let's not ever forget this moment."

"How could we?" she asked.

Christopher hugged them both and said, "Do you want to know how many animals are on my list now? More than fifty!"

"That's wonderful, son," Hank said. He looked over at Ginny and smiled one of the most contented smiles she'd ever seen on his face.

When they returned home, Hank began thinking about what his next project should be. He'd had some offers before he left for Africa, but nothing he was overly excited about. Now, he could feel everything shifting around him. It wasn't just that the nature of the films was changing; it was more the fact that the New Hollywood he'd played such a major part in defining in the mid-1960s was now a thing of the past. Many would say Hank had thoroughly *reinvented* film music, a claim difficult to make for any other film composer. To this day, he is one of only a handful who ever became a household name.

The New Hollywood was a film era in which the director played a bigger role than the studio in the creative direction of things, but this had given way to a much more corporate Hollywood by the late '80s. From this emerged a system that downplayed the singular vision of a film's creator, and by extension all the other contributions of key creative people as well, as the studios opted instead to micromanage and make decisions by committee.

Hank often voiced his dissatisfaction with these unwelcome changes to Ginny, who saw many parallels to the changes that led her to stop working as a session singer. When she first started out, she loved the camaraderie of singing harmony with other singers. But that entire approach changed into one in which recording one voice at a time became the preferred method, so that they could then be "overdubbed" and later mixed with other voices, giving engineers more control. She completely understood and shared Hank's frustration.

"They have people making creative decisions who have no experience at all. The whole industry has changed," he told her.

"I know it," she said.

Blake, Hank's friend and longtime collaborator, was getting caught up trying to operate in an industry that was no longer recognizable to him. After Hank suffered through the process of working on *Ghost Dad* in 1990, which was called one of the worst films of the decade despite being directed by the immensely gifted Sidney Poitier, Hank signed on to do *Switch* in 1991 with Blake. It was particularly difficult for Hank to see Blake bending to the will of young studio executives, who were only interested in gaining more power for themselves and more leverage in creative decision-making, despite their lack of creative talent. Suddenly, film was being treated just like any other product: the focus was entirely on the bottom line instead of on making great stories that would succeed in the marketplace based on the merits of the material and the collective creative output.

Filmmaking had always had a great deal of risk attached to it, but Hank felt that the way to mitigate the risk was not to bring in a bunch of young kids with a corporate mentality. He knew it was a business, but he was accustomed to achieving success through his hard work of learning the craft. If it had ever really been 50 percent show, 50 percent business, the equation was now much more lopsided, in favor of business. Hank feared that the approach of second-guessing every single creative decision would do nothing to advance the cause of quality filmmaking. After all, the executives were tasked with hiring the key creative people and, beyond that, should have allowed those professionals to do their jobs, rather than tell them how to do those jobs every step of the way.

On *Switch*, a battle erupted between the studio, Blake, and Hank about music for the opening of the film. Hank had written something very fitting to play over a long shot moving through clouds that simply floated behind the opening credits. Hank felt that, with this minimalist imagery, the music needed to signal to the audience what kind of film and story they were about to see. But in an effort to appease the studio, Blake overruled Hank and used Joni Mitchell's "Both Sides Now" instead of Hank's opening piece. Blake's calculation was one based on self-preservation—he knew that if he wanted to keep working, he was going to have to play by the new rules, as much as he hated them. Aside from the personal sting of having his theme rejected, Hank felt the song just didn't fit. While some of the lyrics may have hinted at the plot, it just didn't make sense. Joni's song was melancholic and earnest, and had no place in a comedy about a cheating man killed by three of his ex-girlfriends who is given the chance to come back—as a woman—to make amends. The song would have been put to much better use in a serious drama. Hank guessed that Joni Mitchell was also pressured to put her poignant and beautiful song in a movie in which it really didn't fit for the sake of promoting it. Hank had always held to higher standards and he was not about to lower them now. The 1993 film *Son of the Pink Panther*, with Blake at the helm, would be Hank's final feature film score.

In the early 1990s, Hank returned to RCA after many years, under the moniker of the Mancini Pops Orchestra. Ever the music pioneer, the album *Mancini in Surround: Mostly Monsters, Murders & Mysteries* was the first album ever to be recorded and mixed for Dolby surround sound. In 1991, the Mancini Pops Orchestra released *Cinema Italiano: Music of Ennio Morricone & Nino Rota*. Then, in 1992, he put out his final two albums, also with the Mancini Pops Orchestra: *As Time Goes By and Other Classic Movie Love Songs* and *Top Hat*. As he played the love songs album at home for Ginny for the first time, she asked him for a dance in the living room.

"Enrico Mancini, would you like to escort me to my fiftieth high school reunion?" she asked.

"I can't think of anything more I'd like to do, Miss O'Connor," he answered with a wink.

Hank and Ginny had always found ways to have fun, and after all their years together, Ginny was looking forward to showing off her husband to her high school class.

One corner of the music world in which Hank had not yet had the opportunity to work was musical theater, despite it being a dream of his for a very long time. For thirteen years, after the success of the film *Victor/Victoria*, Blake Edwards continued to renew its theatrical rights at great personal expense, until his producing partner finally told him it was time to make something happen with it or let it go. Blake and Julie Andrews both very much wanted to bring *Victor/Victoria* to Broadway. It was a complicated process, as new songs had to be written and others reworked to fit the new structure of a stage adaptation. New York had historically frowned upon Hollywood film directors who strayed onto this turf, and this project was no exception. It would prove to be a formidable challenge for Blake to make his first outing in this arena at seventy-one years old. Julie was fifty-eight and eager to return to her theater roots, reprising her role from the film. Blake's initial plan for the stage version was to retain two of the songs from the film, but that number eventually became five.

This made things extra tricky for Hank and lyricist Leslie Bricusse, who, instead of writing for a finished film scene, were trying to write songs for a stage play that was still in the process of being crafted. As a team, they'd had a dry run at this some years earlier in 1978, when they worked together on a musical adaptation of the George Bernard Shaw play *Major Barbara*, the story of a high-society woman who joined the Salvation Army. All indications were that Julie Andrews would star in it, but after a great deal of haggling with the Shaw estate over how Shaw's lines would be handled if used in song, as opposed to how they had already been cleared for use in speech, Hank and Leslie decided to walk away from the project and left behind fifteen original songs.

They had learned important lessons from this experience that they were putting to good use now. But it seemed that Hank's stamina was not what it once was. While working one day, Hank was hit by a wave of fatigue.

"Les, do you mind if we take a short break?" he asked.

Leslie could see that Hank was having some trouble breathing. "Yes, of course. Can I get you anything?"

"I'll be okay. I just need a few minutes." But the truth was, Hank had noticed his energy levels had dropped precipitously in the last weeks. "I'm just so tired. I don't feel rested even after I sleep," he told Leslie.

Hank told Ginny what he was experiencing. He was not usually the one rushing off to the doctor's office; his symptoms scared Ginny and he could see it on her face. She took him to the family physician, who discovered blood clots in his lungs.

"That does seem like it would make it hard to breathe," Hank said to the doctor and Ginny, trying to put a lighter face on things.

Ginny followed the doctor out to the hallway to talk, and Hank didn't find out until later what the doctor had told her—that he had inoperable cancer of the pancreas and it was affecting his liver. He only had months to live.

He was hospitalized for a few days, sent home, and went right back to work on the musical. Despite the dire diagnosis, he never lost the ability to lose himself in his work. Two months after his diagnosis, he gave an interview to *The Globe and Mail* in Toronto, for which the headline read, "Mancini Works on Score Despite Cancer Diagnosis." He spoke extensively about how much he still loved to work, and said work was the best therapy he knew. He said he had every intention of finishing the score for *Victor/Victoria*. "It's a strange thing. When I write, I don't think of anything but what I'm doing. I don't feel any different when I'm writing. I just go," he said.

He sincerely believed there could still be time for a miracle—to see the musical make it to Broadway. He continued to work toward this goal as much as his physical body would allow. As the news started to make its way around amongst his friends and colleagues, Hank got a phone call from Gene Lees, his friend and co-writer of Hank's autobiography, *Did They Mention the Music?* That title references his days at Universal, when the staff of composers would work on films as a team and, after the initial screenings for studio brass, would want to know if the powers that be mentioned the music. Gene knew he was the one in the position of attempting to provide comfort, but instead, the opposite occurred. Hank told him he was feeling very serene about the whole thing and paraphrased a quote from the J. D. Salinger story *For Esmé—with Love and Squalor*, about a World War II soldier about to go into combat. "Your number is either up or it's not," he told Gene.

Indeed, the people around Hank began to notice his ability to simultaneously hold two incompatible things in his head and heart—the knowledge that his life was coming to an end, and complete grace in the face of it. It seemed, once again, that he was embodying the idea of the grace note—those nonessential notes that bring something to a melody or harmony, to make it sound *more human*, as some would say.

Hank decided to write a couple letters to "his guys," many of the union musicians he'd employed over the years. The first one he wrote implored them to take better care of their health, telling them in no uncertain terms, "In three months, I'll be out of here." The second letter was to say goodbye.

Hank gave his last interview on the back porch of his home to entertainment historian and Mancini fan Leonard Maltin. "I had CAT-scans, dog-scans, you name it. I'm not going to fight it," he told Leonard. "I feel very much at peace for some reason. It's somewhat of a cleansing because there's less buzzing around in your head of things to do and think about. There is more focus now and, jeez, I've been trying to do that for forty years in this business."

Monica and Felice were not at all happy to hear their father talk about "not fighting it." They were not ready to let him go. There had been no warning that they could lose their devoted father to an essentially undetectable disease—they saw him as larger than life and timeless, just as his legion of fans did. They feverishly researched alternative treatments not yet approved in the U.S. but that might be available in Europe or Mexico. Ginny did her best to comfort them when it became more obvious that Hank was losing strength every day.

"It's hard to sit still when you think there's something that can be done," Monica told Hank and Ginny.

"I appreciate everything you kids do for me," Hank told her.

"But it's not enough. Nothing will be enough unless we can stop this thing," she said, her voice beginning to quake.

Chris went on national television and said, "We really are just dedicated to giving our father the best of ourselves right now."

Hank told a reporter in a phone interview, "What matters most is my family and friends. That's it. Regardless of what happens, things have never been better in my life. I am very much at peace."

A couple months after the diagnosis, Hank found himself surrounded by all his wonderful friends and family at his seventieth birthday celebration. It was a fitting charity gala on behalf of someone who had earned the respect of so many people over a lifetime, and he was surrounded by his colleagues in the music and film industries.

Hank had always set a powerful example for his contemporaries, given the fact that anyone who ever attained such a high level of success was at risk for becoming arrogant or out of touch. Everyone around Hank had been inspired by how down to earth he was, by virtue of the fact that he never forgot where he came from. No matter how famous, wealthy, or celebrated he became, he always identified with musicians all the way to the last chair in the orchestra. At no point in his journey did he ever take anything for granted or fail to recognize his mentors who helped him achieve all that he did. His friends showed their appreciation of Hank and all of his admirable qualities by giving generously—to the tune of two million dollars—to support his ongoing philanthropic mission. The money was split evenly to benefit Hank's Young Musician's Foundation, UCLA Center for the Performing Arts, and L.A. County High School for the Arts. Ginny, the ultimate party planner, chose UCLA's Pauley Pavilion to hold the three thousand guests, for whom John Williams conducted a Hollywood pickup orchestra, and where pink paw prints guided guests to their seats. Tiffany & Co. donated one of the party favors—a demitasse cup decorated with the notes to "Moon River."

No one knew it then, but that night was the last time Hank would ever be in front of an audience. He said a few words from his seat, not feeling steady enough to go up on stage. The guests all knew they were taking part in a very special night. So many of the people Hank had met on his journey did a laudable job of making sure their friend knew how much he meant to them. Quincy Jones took the stage and made a very moving toast to Hank, speaking candidly about how much he felt he owed part of his career to him.

"Hank's tireless support of me, as a young black man trying to break into film composing, made all the difference in the world," he said. "It simply may never have happened without his support and friendship. I love you, brother."

Quincy turned to face the orchestra and raised his baton to conduct "Peter Gunn." Luciano Pavarotti, who made the trip from Italy to sing "Happy Birthday" in the style of Verdi to Hank, called Hank his "*grande amico*." He went on to perform for forty minutes.

Then Andy Williams graced the stage. "The wonders of Henry Mancini will be heard in every corner of the world right up to the minute this planet cools and shrinks to the size of an eighth note," he said. "Happy birthday to one of the nicest men I have ever known, as well as the most devious sense of humor."

This gave Hank a good chuckle. Andy then sang "Moon River" and was followed by Julie Andrews singing "Two for the Road," which had always been Ginny's favorite of Hank's songs. The lyrics took on a different meaning that night, knowing how near the end was for Hank.

If you're feeling fancy free,
Come wander through the world with me,
And any place we chance to be,
Will be a rendezvous.
Two for the road,
We'll travel through the years,
Collecting precious memories,
Selecting souvenirs
And living life the way we please.
In the summertime the sun will shine,
In winter we'll drink summer wine,
And any day that you are mine

Will be a lovely day.
As long as love still wears a smile,
I know that we'll be two for the road,
And that's a long, long while.

Just a day after the party at UCLA, Ginny and Monica took Hank to a studio to record "With Love" for Rich Warren, the new theme for a children's pediatric AIDS awareness campaign. It was physically painful for Hank to play piano—he had a hard time getting off the couch, but he was determined to fulfill this commitment. His other final project was a film called *A Memory for Tino*, based on author Leo Buscaglia's notion that "the most we can give to anyone and the easiest thing we have to give is our time." On a title card at the end of film is a dedication:

This film is dedicated to
the memory of the composer Henry Mancini,
who gave and gave and gave . . .

Two months after celebrating his seventieth birthday, Hank succumbed to his cancer on June 14, 1994. Leslie Bricusse wrote, "At UCLA's Pauley Pavilion, Henry made a quiet but moving speech and took his final bows like the modest man he was. As it says in his most beloved song, 'Moon River,' he crossed in style."

More than the musical legacy he left behind was the family who absolutely adored him, which, to Hank, was the true measure of the value of his life. Friends had heard him say this over the years—that more people should think about the way others will continue to tell your story long after you're gone. Hank once told one of his musician friends who wondered why, with so much repertoire, Hank always returned to one piece over and over again, always placing it near the beginning of the show—the theme from *Mr. Lucky*. When he asked Hank about it, his response was, "Because I'm Mr. Lucky. My life is in that tune."

Ginny told NPR, "I was lucky enough to be married to him for forty-seven incredibly wonderful years. He was great, not only as a musician, but just the greatest human being. I've never known anyone quite like Henry, whose temperament was so gentle. He was a gentle giant." At no point would Ginny ever not feel him in her heart daily as she carried on doing the important work they began together. Monica decided she no longer wanted to ski, knowing it would never be the same without him.

If anyone had ever entertained the notion that Hank and his inimitable style would not continue to be in demand by the next generation of the best film directors, they need only look to the fact that, just before his diagnosis, he was approached by the critically acclaimed director Tim Burton to score his film *Ed Wood*, starring Johnny Depp, about the real-life eccentric director of the 1950s. Hank had recently signed with a new agent, who was working on this deal, and it seemed like he was entering a second golden era of his career. But the new era never came to be.

He'd told Christopher some years earlier that what he wanted more than anything was for the whole family to be together at the millennium, a bridge he would have liked to cross. That did not come to pass, but Hank was never one to complain. He never got caught up worrying about his own legacy, nor did he give himself too much credit for writing some of the most iconic themes and melodies ever recorded. However, he was fairly confident that he had left the world a better place than he'd found it. The bridge connecting West Aliquippa to greater Aliquippa was renamed the Henry Mancini Memorial Bridge before Hank's passing and serves as a symbol of this.

Hank himself was a bridge—he connected musical styles, he brought people together and fought for equality, he gave to the next generation, and, most importantly, he bridged his own success with humility and humanity. Hank understood, almost better than anyone, that music is a universal language with tremendous power to unite people. As Italian as his heritage is, Henry Mancini *is* American music.

About the Author

Stacia Raymond is a freelance writer and editor based in Southern California. With over fifteen years of experience in the film and television industry, Stacia's body of work includes fiction, non-fiction, and ghostwriting for clients in the fields of music, film, and technology. Stacia's television writing has been produced by CBS, Paramount, and Lifetime, and she has developed projects with Showtime and ABC Family. In 2013, she was awarded a Fellowship with the Puglia Film Commission as part of a program to bring more production to the Southern Italian region. Stacia holds a B.A. in Communications from The American University and an M.F.A. in Professional Writing from the University of Southern California. She is a member of the Writers Guild of America and the American Society of Composers, Authors, and Publishers. She is currently working on her first book for children, *The Carol of the Ornaments*, and maintains a blog of personal essays focusing on the serendipitous nature of everything.

NOW AVAILABLE FROM THE MENTORIS PROJECT

America's Forgotten Founding Father
A Novel Based on the Life of Filippo Mazzei
by Rosanne Welch

A. P. Giannini—The People's Banker
by Francesca Valente

Building Heaven's Ceiling
A Novel Based on the Life of Filippo Brunelleschi
by Joe Cline

Christopher Columbus: His Life and Discoveries
by Mario Di Giovanni

The Faithful
A Novel Based on the Life of Giuseppe Verdi
by Collin Mitchell

Fermi's Gifts
A Novel Based on the Life of Enrico Fermi
by Kate Fuglei

God's Messenger
The Astounding Achievements of Mother Cabrini
A Novel Based on the Life of Mother Frances X. Cabrini
by Nicole Gregory

Harvesting the American Dream
A Novel Based on the Life of Ernest Gallo
by Karen Richardson

Humble Servant of Truth
A Novel Based on the Life of Thomas Aquinas
by Margaret O'Reilly

Leonardo's Secret
A Novel Based on the Life of Leonardo da Vinci
by Peter David Myers

Marconi and His Muses
A Novel Based on the Life of Guglielmo Marconi
by Pamela Winfrey

Saving the Republic
A Novel Based on the Life of Marcus Cicero
by Eric D. Martin

Soldier, Diplomat, Archaeologist
A Novel Based on the Bold Life of Louis Palma di Cesnola
by Peg A. Lamphier

COMING IN 2018 FROM THE MENTORIS PROJECT

A Novel Based on the Life of Cosimo de' Medici
A Novel Based on the Life of Maria Montessori
A Novel Based on the Life of Niccolò Machiavelli
A Novel Based on the Life of Scipio Africanus

FUTURE TITLES FROM THE MENTORIS PROJECT

Cycles of Wealth
Fulfilling the Promise of California
A Novel Based on the Life of Alessandro Volta
A Novel Based on the Life of Amerigo Vespucci
A Novel Based on the Life of Andrea Doria
A Novel Based on the Life of Andrea Palladio
A Novel Based on the Life of Angelo Dundee
A Novel Based on the Life of Antonin Scalia
A Novel Based on the Life of Antonio Meucci
A Novel Based on the Life of Artemisia Gentileschi
A Novel Based on the Life of Buzzie Bavasi
A Novel Based on the Life of Cesare Becaria
A Novel Based on the Life of the Explorer John Cabot
A Novel Based on the Life of Federico Fellini
A Novel Based on the Life of Frank Capra
A Novel Based on the Life of Galileo Galilei
A Novel Based on the Life of Giuseppe Garibaldi
A Novel Based on the Life of Guido d'Arezzo
A Novel Based on the Life of Harry Warren

A Novel Based on the Life of Judge John J. Sirica
A Novel Based on the Life of Laura Bassi
A Novel Based on the Life of Leonard Covello
A Novel Based on the Life of Leonardo Fibonacci
A Novel Based on the Life of Luca Pacioli
A Novel Based on the Life of Maria Gaetana Agnesi
A Novel Based on the Life of Mario Andretti
A Novel Based on the Life of Mario Cuomo
A Novel Based on the Life of Peter Rodino
A Novel Based on the Life of Pietro Belluschi
A Novel Based on the Life of Rita Levi-Montalcini
A Novel Based on the Life of Saint Augustine of Hippo
A Novel Based on the Life of Saint Francis of Assisi
A Novel Based on the Life of Vince Lombardi

For more information on these titles and
The Mentoris Project, please visit
www.mentorisproject.org.

CPSIA information can be obtained
at www.ICGtesting.com
Printed in the USA
LVHW112354261018
595028LV00001B/26/P